Smith's MONTHLY

*Every Month Original
Novels, Stories, and Articles*

USA Today Bestselling Writer
Dean Wesley Smith

I0553968

TABLE OF CONTENTS

SHORT STORIES

FULL NOVEL

NONFICTION

Smith's Monthly Issue #43

Dean Wesley Smith

Introduction
IT'S ALL IN THE DETAILS

For some reason, I got interested in stagecoaches right before I started the Thunder Mountain novel in this issue.

And not just any stagecoach, but a Concord stagecoach, considered the top of the line back in the 1850s through the early 1900s.

Everyone knows what Concord stagecoaches look like because of all the movies. Egg-shaped in general, with a place for the driver and guard to sit up front, railings around the top where people could sit or luggage could be stored, and a lump on the back that was for storing luggage as well.

If in a movie a stage needed to be robbed, it would be a Concord, even though there were hundreds of other types.

Now, so far in all my Thunder Mountain novels, no character would think of riding in a stagecoach. My characters all rode horses. Stagecoaches were rough rides at best and I knew that so I never put my character in one.

If you ever get a chance for a stagecoach ride at a fair or something, take it. And remember that you are riding on flat, level ground. Imagine the coach tipped sideways going over rocks and bouncing through ruts. Nothing at all comfortable about the ride, which is one of the many reasons trains and then cars took over so quickly.

The Concords also had a special system to try to make the ride smoother. They had large bands of thick leather that gave the coach a rocking motion under the bouncing.

Imagine being on a very small boat in rough seas with something pounding the bottom of the coach every few feet and tipping the entire thing one way and then the other. Yup, passengers got motion sick and bruised in even the shortest rides.

A woman and a man, complete strangers, sitting on a bench seat in a stagecoach, ended up knowing each other very well by the time the trip was over

Thanks for the Support

Dean Wesley Smith

because they were always tossed together by the rough roads.

I think what got me interested in the Concord stagecoach were all the myths around them. Every western movie has a stage pulling into town or being robbed or the beautiful woman arriving and stepping down looking wonderful.

No reality there at all. Even the Concords with their leather blinds over the windows got their passengers covered in dust.

In the Thunder Mountain novels, I try to keep the details clear and crisp and as accurate as I can manage when it comes to the Old West. So I thought I would tackle the myth of the Concord stagecoach. Both in the past and in today's time. Thus the novel *Dry Creek Crossing*.

And by the way, right where I have Dry Creek Crossing in this book, there really was a wagon road that went across the stream called Dry Creek that is west and to the north a little from Boise, Idaho. Only the creek was seldom dry, if ever. No idea why or how it got the name Dry Creek.

And another point about details. Rattlesnakes make an appearance in both of the last two Thunder Mountain novels, including the novel in this issue. Rattlesnakes were very much a part of the Old West.

Like I said, I try to get the details right in these Thunder Mountain novels. I hope you enjoy reading it as much as I did writing it.

—Dean Wesley Smith
July 31st, 2017

Now Available!

Five-Story Collections in Some of Dean Wesley Smith's Most Popular Series. Find them at your favorite booksellers!

Coming Next Issue in *Smith's Monthly*

BURN CARD
A Cold Poker Gang Novel

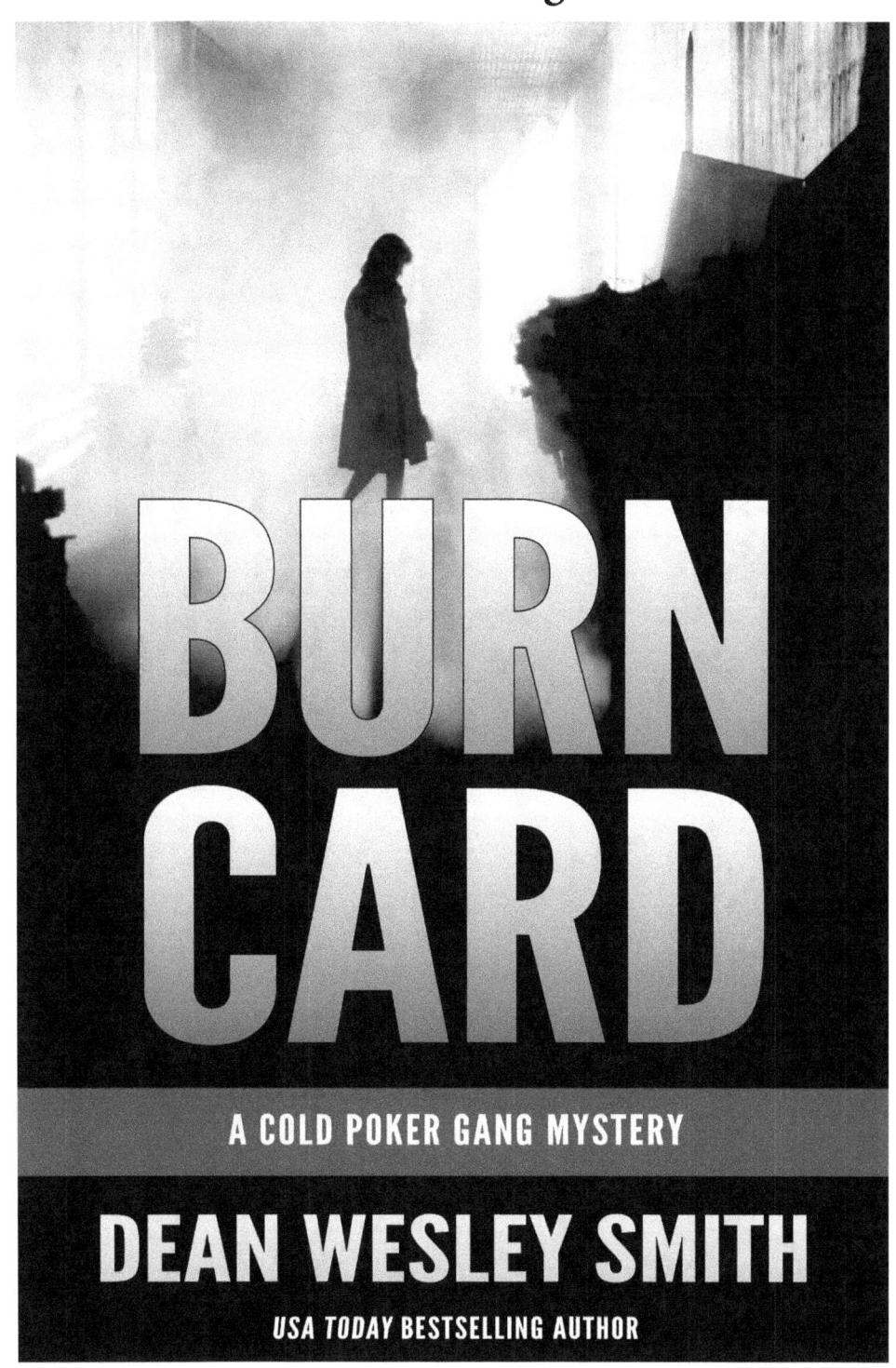

A COLD POKER GANG MYSTERY

DEAN WESLEY SMITH

USA TODAY BESTSELLING AUTHOR

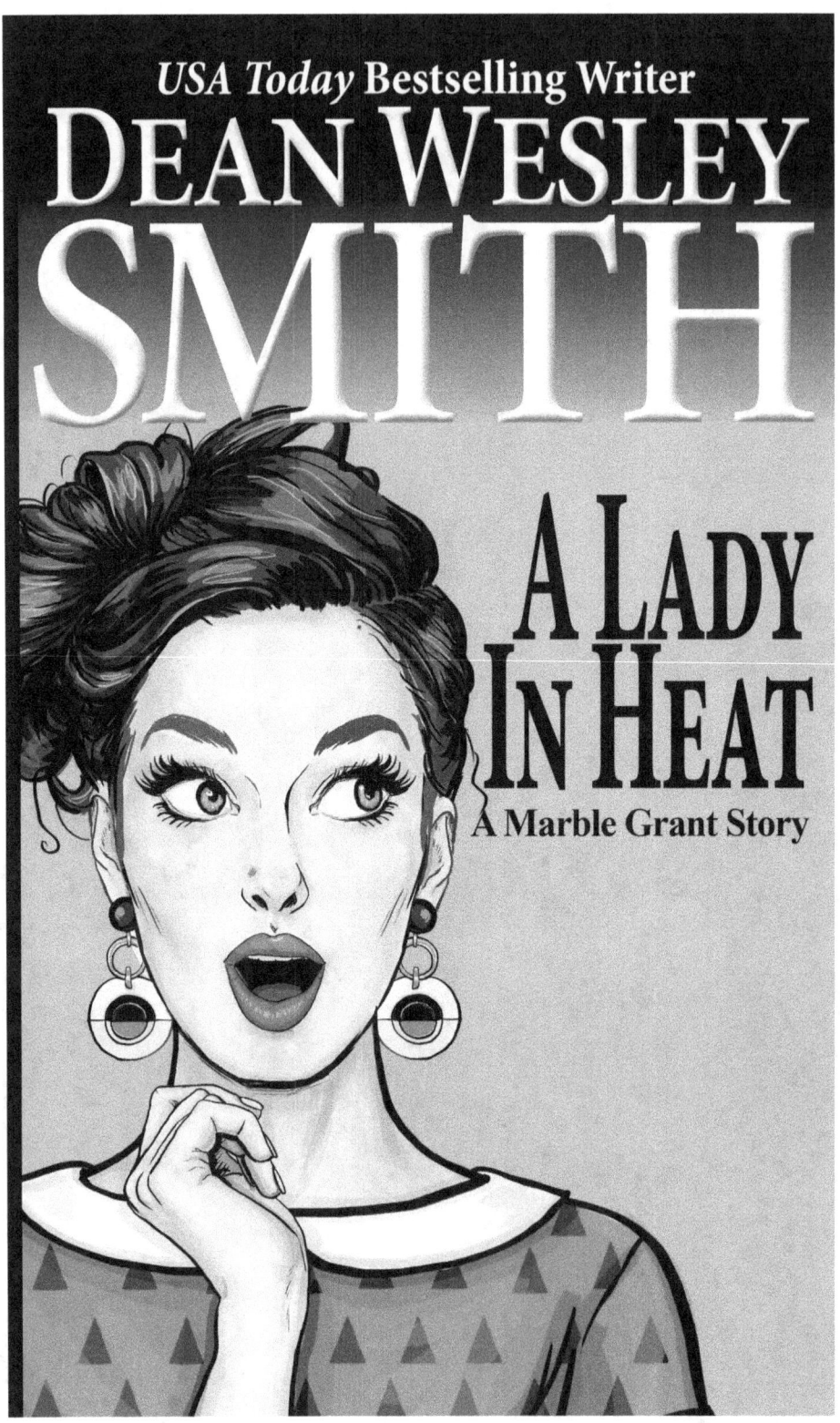

USA *Today* Bestselling Writer

DEAN WESLEY SMITH

A LADY
IN HEAT

A Marble Grant Story

Marble Grant and her partner Sim stumble on a beautiful, drop-dead sexy woman moments before she actually drops dead.

That sort of kills all the fun in the moment.

While the Fremont Street Experience swirls around the three ghosts, Marble works to figure out why the woman's ride in a bright-light tunnel seemed late.

No telling what might happen when Marble Grant and Sim stride to the rescue.

A LADY IN HEAT
A Marble Grant Story

FROM WHERE I stood off to one side of the Fremont Street Experience, leaning against the stone wall of the Golden Nugget Casino, I could watch a woman with long blonde hair, a tight white blouse, jeans, and expensive tennis shoes.

She was hot, not temperature hot, since the night was a comfortable seventy degrees. I mean drop-dead sexy hot. Long blonde hair, huge brown eyes, and a smile that could give a dead man an erection.

And she looked drunk.

Staggering drunk, in a sexy, hot way.

Around me and my partner, Sim, the craziness of downtown Las Vegas swirled like a midway at a carnival. An X-rated carnival with a twist of New Orleans French Quarter tossed in. There were men wearing G-strings who shouldn't ever wear G-strings, women with basically nothing on willing to pose with anyone for a few bucks right beside every cartoon character imaginable.

I was pretty sure that in the books Sleeping Beauty didn't have to compete with Amazon-sized women beside her wearing armor from the waist down.

Three bands played along the street about a block or so apart with crowds dancing in front of the stages.

And everyone carried a drink.

The entire four-block-long street party was covered by a ninety-foot-high dome of lights. Making it impossible to walk a straight line down the big mall were more small booths and bars than should be crammed into four blocks of space.

Overhead people screamed as they went flying by on a zip-line, just under the dome roof. And the half-dozen major casinos that fronted the Experience all had their doors wide open like hungry mouths welcoming in the food they called tourists.

I honestly loved the Experience, even as tacky and stupid as it was. It had a life to it every night, seven nights a week. And to ghosts like me and Sim, feeling alive was important.

Besides, we only lived about three blocks from the Experience, so wandering through here regularly was something we just did.

"You looking at what I'm looking at?" Sim asked as the hot blonde sort of stumbled into a guy with his wife and daughter in tow. The blonde said something to the poor guy who looked flustered and the guy's wife looked shocked and yanked the guy away.

Sim glanced over at me and smiled. "I think she just propositioned that poor guy."

"I think you might be right," I said, laughing.

"Think she might be interested in two women ghosts?" Sim asked.

"I know I would be interested in finding out what she is thinking," I said, laughing, as we both started across the mall toward her.

When trying to go from one place to another through crowds, we had three choices. We could either walk through people and get glimpses of all of their thoughts and memories, we could try to avoid as many as we could, which meant some tricky side-stepping and ducking moves, or we could just teleport, or jump as we called it, to the other side.

When working the Experience, Sim and I liked to try to avoid. More fun and some pretty good exercise.

I reached the hot blonde first and faded inside her. A few seconds later Sim joined me.

But I didn't notice exactly when Sim joined me because this woman was the horniest woman I had ever seen. It was like waves and waves of desire cascaded through her mind.

I damn near had an orgasm just trying to get a grip on what I was sensing in this woman's mind.

"Holy shit!" Sim said, breathing hard.

The woman was named Maryalice without a hyphen and she was in Vegas alone, trying to make herself forget her boyfriend.

"We got to get her off this street," I said to Sim through what felt like an intense red haze inside the woman's mind.

"No kidding," Sim said, seeming to shout even though I could hear her fine. "She's on some sort of drug."

I could feel the woman's heart racing, her breath getting shorter and shorter. She was just about to overdose right here in the middle of this crowd.

"Get her over against the casino wall and I'll get help," I said to Sim.

I stepped out of the woman, shuddering at how the entire sexual feelings still sort of hung around me like moss off a tree. That might take some release to clear later tonight with Sim. Wow.

A handsome young security cop was about fifty feet away. I jumped into him and got him turned and headed through the crowd toward the woman at full run.

He was young and gay and loved the strangeness of the crowds at the Experience as well. His partner worked in one of the nearby casinos and they had a dog named Spot because it had been hard to apartment train.

Sim had gotten the hot blonde over to the wall and had her sitting on the concrete.

Her face looked sickly white and her eyes were closed.

I had the cop call for emergency medical help before he even got to the woman, making him understand the woman was overdosing on something.

Sim hadn't appeared from the woman yet.

So when the cop kneeled down beside the woman who now looked like she was passing out, I went back inside of her.

Sim was doing her best to hold the woman together.

But we both knew almost instantly we were too late. This woman's body was shutting down and shutting down hard.

"We need to get out of here now," I said to Sim. "We don't want to be in here when she dies."

"What would happen if we were?" Sim asked as I joined her to try to keep the woman's heart pumping just a little longer.

"We'll figure that out later," I said.

I knew there were many reasons I loved Sim so much. But one was her fight and the fact she just wasn't willing to let go against all odds.

But at the last possible second, Sim did and both of us got out of the dying woman's body just as she took her last breath.

We stepped back and leaned against the wall and out of the way as paramedics arrived and started CPR. A half-circle of gawkers formed around them as they worked.

But Sim and I both knew Maryalice was dead.

Dead far before she had really gotten a chance to do much living.

Damn it. If we had gotten to her sooner we might have been able to save her.

Then a voice beside us said simply, "Well that sucks. All I wanted to do was get laid."

Both Sim and I spun around to face Maryalice's ghost, staring down at her own body being worked over by the paramedics. The cop that I had fetched was watching, his face in shock.

"I wonder if he would be interested in doing it with a dead girl?" Maryalice said, moving toward the cop.

"Hang on," I said.

Maryalice turned and looked at me, then at her body on the ground, then back at me. "You are dead too?"

"We both are," Sim said.

"You two were in my head trying to save me, weren't you?"

I nodded.

"Nice of you."

"What did you take to cause that?" Sim asked, pointing at the body on the ground with the oxygen mask over her face and someone pumping her chest.

"Not a clue," Maryalice said, shrugging, which made her wonderful breasts do wonderful things. "My old boyfriend gave the pills to me at one point to try to calm my inhibitions. Never tried them until tonight. He was such a bastard I should have known they would do something like this to me."

"Or maybe you took too many?" I asked, smiling at her.

Both Sim and I knew that was what had happened. Maryalice had taken one, didn't feel anything, so took three more with a glass of vodka right before heading for the Experience.

"Yeah, might have done that," she said, laughing. "Too late now I suppose."

She glanced around. "You two the only ghosts around these parts? And why am I still here? Aren't I supposed to be riding some magic light off into another world?"

"You are," Sim said, nodding.

I was worried about that, actually. Was this woman going to be another Agent?

At that point the medics on the ground put some sort of tube down Maryalice's throat and started pumping out the contents of her stomach. After they did that, they kept up CPR and oxygen.

"Well, that's gross," Maryalice said, staring at what was being done to her body.

"They are still trying to save you," Sim said.

Suddenly I realized why this woman's light hadn't arrived yet. She wasn't completely disconnected from her body yet, which meant she might be able to be saved.

"What's your old boyfriend's name and where does he live exactly?" I asked.

"Why? Think we can go haunt him?"

"No, I want to find out what the pill was you took," I said. "And I need to do it quickly."

She shrugged and gave me the address in Missoula, Montana and what he looked like and his favorite bar if he wasn't home.

Sim nodded to me that she would watch Maryalice, and I jumped to Missoula.

The guy was a slob and his place smelled of old food, too much garbage, and sweat socks.

He was on a recliner watching television and drinking a beer.

I went inside him.

I was stunned that actually he was a pretty good guy. His name was Bobby, an engineering student, and had been really in love with Maryalice when she left him because he liked sex a little more than she seemed to.

And I had seen that Maryalice really loved him as well, but didn't want to disappoint him by not being good enough at sex for him.

The two were so uptight about it, they couldn't even talk.

I had expected this guy to be a real pig for giving her pills, but turns out he was just as confused about the entire sex thing as she was.

I quickly found the name of the medication she had taken and jumped back to Vegas.

I winked at Sim and then jumped back into the young cop's mind. I quickly made him believe that Maryalice had told him what she had taken and he needed to tell the paramedics at once.

He leaned down and told the paramedics the name of the pill. One of them asked, "Are you sure?"

"She said she took four of them," I made him say.

Then I left him with that clear memory of talking with her and jumped out.

With that information, the paramedics went into even more of a frenzied action.

"Think they might save my sorry ass?" Maryalice said.

"I think you have a damn fine ass," Sim said.

"I do too," I said, smiling at her.

Maryalice laughed and blushed a little. "You know, I don't normally swing toward women, but for you two I might make an exception."

"Now I'm getting hot," Sim said, pretending to fan herself.

"You know," I said to Maryalice, "your boyfriend is a really nice guy and misses you and really isn't worried about your sex life. He just wants you for who you are."

"How do you know that?" Maryalice asked, staring at me.

"Just spent a few seconds inside his head to get the name of the medication he gave you."

"Oh," Maryalice said.

"He finds you as hot as we do. More than likely that's why you thought he wanted sex too much."

Maryalice blushed again. "Actually, I wanted it as much if not more than he did, but was too embarrassed to tell him, like a fool."

"And we know you love him as well," Sim said.

Maryalice looked all misty-eyed. "I do."

"Then tell him that," I said. "And then jump him and ride him like a bucking bronco in a rodeo."

"How about first you climb back into that hot body of yours there," Sim said, "and give this a real fight."

"And tell Bobby you love him when you see him," I said. "Promise me?"

Maryalice nodded. "How do I get back into that mess?"

"Just go over there and sink down into yourself," Sim said. "I'll take you back inside, get you settled."

"Thanks," Maryalice said. "This has been one whacked out dream. Hope I remember it?"

"You will," Sim said.

Sim pointed to me. "That's Marble, I'm Sim. Name your and Bobby's kids after us when the time comes."

"I'll do that," Maryalice said.

With that Sim took her hand and the two of them went over and sunk down into Maryalice's body.

A moment later the paramedic shouted, "I got a pulse! Get the stretcher ready for transport."

I was cheering along with the crowd watching.

A few moments later the love of my life appeared and came toward me smiling.

"She's going to be fine," Sim said. "But I'm not."

"What's wrong?" I asked.

Sim smiled. "I'm so damn horny I could jump you right here."

She kissed me hard and I kissed her back and after a wonderful, long minute, we came up for air.

"Think anyone would notice us?" I asked.

"That might be half the fun," she said, working to get off my blouse at the same time I worked at hers. "We could put out a tip jar."

"We could be rich," I said.

Sim laughed as we slumped to the ground, frantically working on each other's clothes.

Over fifty people walked right through us over the next forty minutes as Sim and I let off some massive pent-up steam, so to speak.

Some of the people who walked through us would have been appalled.

But most would have just thought it another Fremont Street Experience.

That's why I loved this place so much.

Almost anything goes. After all, it is Vegas.

~

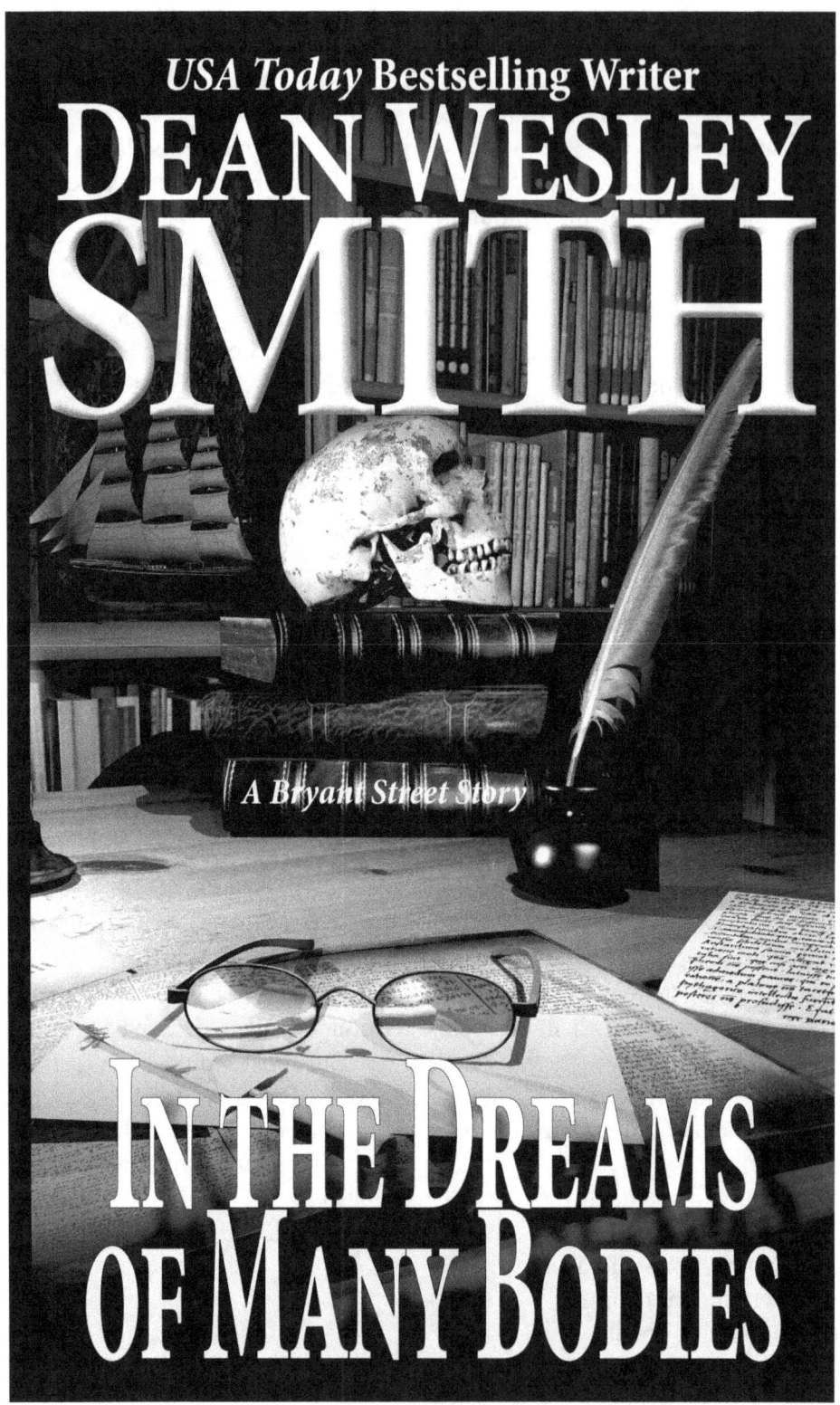

USA *Today* Bestselling Writer

DEAN WESLEY SMITH

A Bryant Street Story

IN THE DREAMS OF MANY BODIES

Harry Stentz killed Cindy Wilson thirty-four years ago.

He even knew exactly where he buried her.

But there, on social media, she appeared with kids and grandkids. And an old picture of herself, the same woman he knew he'd killed.

A twisted short story of a man and a basement on Bryant Street.

IN THE DREAMS OF MANY BODIES
A Bryant Street Story

HARRY STENTZ COULDN'T be looking at the pictures in front of him on his computer.

Those pictures simply couldn't exist.

Cindy Wilson couldn't have kids and grandkids in pictures with her on the internet. She had died thirty-four years before.

He knew that for a fact.

He had killed her.

Yet there she was, smiling at the camera.

Not possible.

He stood up from the computer in his home office and walked into the hallway of his three-bedroom ranch, trying to catch his breath. His slippers shuffled along the hardwood floor as he headed for the kitchen.

He had made a mistake this morning going onto that social media site. He knew better. Now he didn't know what to do.

He had remodeled the kitchen just two years before, putting in state-of-the-art everything. It gleamed and he had kept it shining and clean, even after he cooked a really messy meal. He went to the sink and got a glass of cold water from the tap, then went and sat down at his ornate dining room table.

His kitchen and dining area always had a way of calming him on stressful days.

He had bought the table in case he ever had guests over, but in two years now he hadn't used it for anything but sitting and staring out at his own backyard.

He didn't mind. He loved doing that. The silence was wonderful. It helped him think and plan.

The day was going to be warm and the sprinklers had just shut off, leaving the lawn glistening in the morning sun. He loved green grass and didn't mind paying to keep it green.

He also had his front lawn kept perfectly and the shrubs and flowerbeds along the front of the house always trimmed and bright with colors. He liked to have his neighbors along Bryant Street know he cared for his home.

And that care cost him a pretty penny every month, but he thought it was worth it.

Besides he worked every day in his home. He wrote novels, detective novels to be exact, all with the same detective. Fifty-two so far and they had made him nice money for thirty-two years now.

So since he worked and lived in the home, why wouldn't he care for it more than anything he had ever cared for in his life. It was his safe place, his work place, where all his secrets lay.

He lived alone.

In fact, he had lived his entire life alone once his parents had died when he was seventeen. And he had lived alone for thirty-five years in this house. He had bought it with his grandmother's inheritance money and figured it would be a perfect home base for him.

Her money had also given him enough time to write his detective series of books.

This house was his entire life.

He finished off the glass of water and stood, moving to put the glass in the dishwasher. Then he reached in under the sink and flipped a small, hidden switch there under the front lip.

He heard a faint click.

He closed the cabinet door and turned and headed into the laundry room just off of the garage. To his right was the door leading into the garage, to his left were the washer and dryer and a shelf for supplies.

Under a storage shelf behind the door into the kitchen was another small hidden switch. He flipped it and heard another small click.

Then he went to the shelf unit beside the washer and dryer and moved one bottle on the top shelf over one inch and then slid the shelf unit forward and to one side.

Behind the shelf unit was a wooden door, the same one that had always been on the stairway down to the unfinished basement since he had moved into the house.

In the first year he had hidden the basement door.

The same year he had killed Cindy Wilson.

He went down the wooden steps carefully, letting the door behind him close and the lights in the basement come up bright.

The place had a damp, moldy smell to it, a smell that made his blood race. He had torn up the concrete floor of the basement years before, leaving only a small area of concrete at the foot of the stairs.

On that small patch of concrete was a large leather recliner, worn with use. He loved to just sit in that recliner and stare out over his life's work.

The rest of the basement was open and ran the entire length of the three-bedroom house.

He stopped and stood at the edge of the dirt, looking out over the entire field of beautiful mounds, carefully shaped.

Each mound was a woman he had killed. Fifteen across the far wall under his master bedroom and his second bedroom and master bath.

A second row of fifteen closer.

A third row of fifteen even closer.

He was working on the fourth row. Seven of the fifteen possible mounds had been built.

He also had room for a fifth row. He was still fairly young. He had time.

Each mound had an identical wooden box at the head of the mound and nothing more. But the boxes gave that added detail the space needed.

He stepped out onto a well-worn path on the hard dirt between the mounds and moved to the far row and then went to the left to the very first mound in the basement.

Cindy Wilson lay there. He had buried her there.

He picked up the box at the top of the mound and opened it, pulling out a picture of Cindy Wilson and a ring and a bracelet.

It was the same Cindy Wilson he had just seen on the computer. In fact, the very picture he had in his hands had been on her internet page as what she called a "blast from the past."

She had been a long-haired blonde with a bright smile and a biting sense of humor when he had met her. He had asked her out and she had said no.

She had been nice about it, saying she already had a boyfriend, but it was sweet of him to ask.

He killed her two nights later.

She had been beautiful. He tried to kill only beautiful woman, but a few times he had strayed.

He still kept to his routine. Every woman he killed he buried under a mound in his basement, small bits from her life and a picture or two in a wooden box at the head of the mound.

He put the picture of Cindy Wilson back in the wooden box and closed it, then went back to the staircase and upstairs.

What had been online must have been false. That would teach him to never look at a social media site again.

He had known better.

He went to his office and quickly deleted all references to his presence on that site. Then he backed up all his work files twice and stored them.

Then he shut off his computer completely and unplugged it.

Three hours later he was back from the store with a brand new computer. A computer that had not been contaminated with social media and false information.

He spent the entire afternoon setting up his new computer, then headed out to a late dinner.

At dinner in a fine Italian restaurant that smelled wonderfully of garlic bread and red meat sauce, he met a beautiful black-haired woman named Gina. She waited on him and smiled like she really cared.

He found out she was twenty-six, working on saving to open her own restaurant, and was single. She found out he was a writer and really opened up to him.

He remembered every detail, as he always did.

And he even got a picture of her to remind himself of the evening. She hadn't minded at all.

She would be perfect.

Four days later, in chapter three of his new Detective Harry Stentz novel, she died.

In the basement he dug another mound, with another wooden box.

And soon after his fifty-third novel came out to praise and rave reviews, talking about how realistic it all seemed.

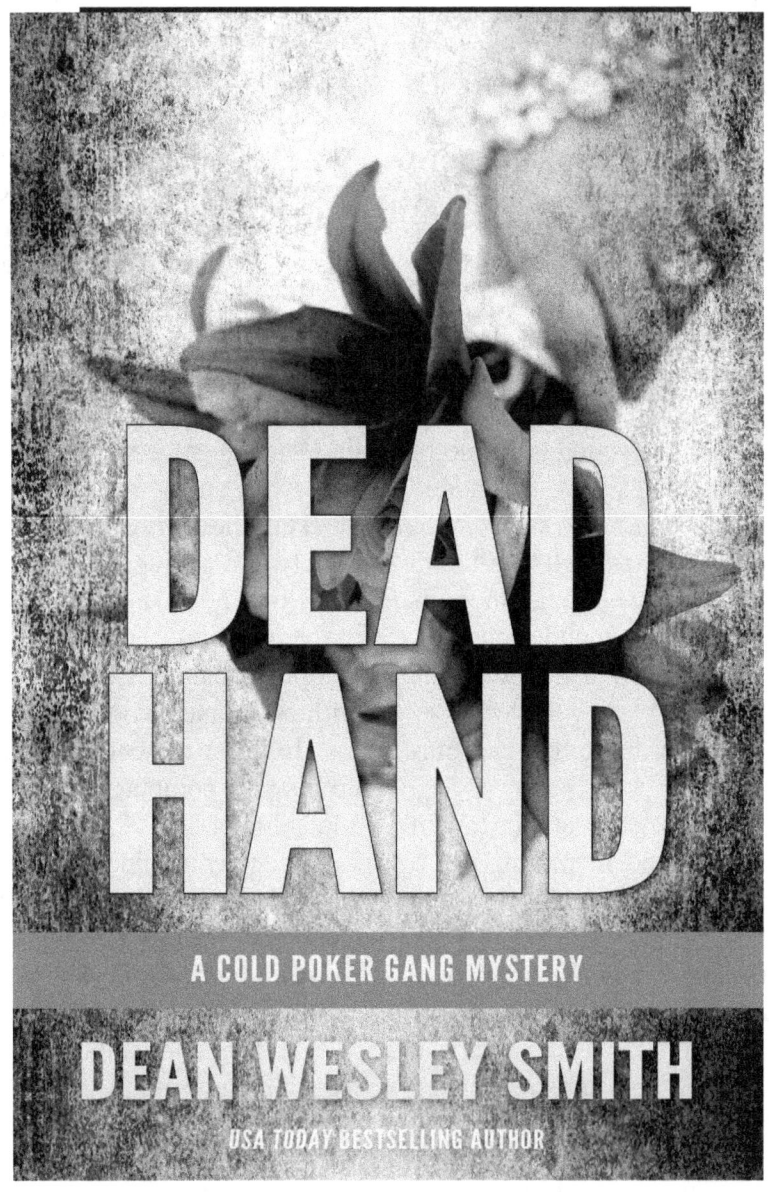

Now Available
from all your favorite booksellers
in trade paper and electronic editions.

Now Available
from all your favorite booksellers
in trade paper and electronic editions.

USA TODAY BESTSELLING AUTHOR

DEAN WESLEY SMITH

COPYRIGHT IN THE MODERN WORLD OF FICTION PUBLISHING

A WMG WRITER'S GUIDE

USA Today bestselling writer Dean Wesley Smith helps writers understand the very nature of their business, how to sell more, and make more money from every story.

Using the metaphor of a magic bakery, copyright becomes easy to understand, and the writing business makes far more sense.

This book functions as a guide to help writers gain more from every story they write, protect their property, and understand how to expand their business into the future.

Clear, easy to read, and full of insights from a forty-year career writer who understands how every story contains magic. Want more sales, more money from your writing? Come on in to The Magic Bakery.

THE MAGIC BAKERY
A WMG Writer's Guide

Part 2 of 2

CHAPTER EIGHT

Doors to the Bakery

Any business must have a way to get into the business.

For example, at our North collectable store here in town you can enter through an interior staircase and climb, or climb an exterior staircase. Both methods take some work for customers and we also have a special entrance in the back that comes in without stairs.

Three entrances. We have the store full of enough cool stuff, we hope it is worth the customer's climb.

So how do readers, publishers, and others get into your bakery to buy your magic pies?

The fun of Magic Bakeries, there are many actual doors.

Far more doors, actually, than you have products in the bakery.

Yeah, a Magic Bakery is a strange place, but it is magical after all.

An example: Say you have written one short story only and published it.

The magic pie that is that short story is sitting on the shelf all by itself. Your bakery is empty and no customers are really going to stop by, even if they happen to find your one story somewhere.

So at that moment in time, your bakery only has a few dozen doors and nothing to hold customers when they arrive.

Why that many doors? Because you have been smart and put the story out wide, meaning Amazon, B&N, Kobo, D2D and so on through all the places D2D and Smashwords distribute to. (I'll talk about paper below.)

So for the sake of simple, say that your one story is for sale at a dozen places.

One story times a dozen places is a dozen ways someone can find your story and thus enter your Magic Bakery.

Every Story is a Door into Your Work

This concept flies in the face of the old myths about writing slow, only doing a book a year or two. Sorry if you are still using one of those myths as an excuse to not sit and write much. You need to figure out how to change that.

Productivity is king in this modern world and the reason is simple. Every story or novel or collection you put out is a doorway to your Magic Bakery and all your other work.

So say I have 300 different products out there in one form or another. (I have more.) Each product is sold wide. So I have about 3,600 doors into my bakery that readers can come through at any

moment. Or movie folks or gaming offers or overseas publishers.

Those doors are all over the world, folks.

This is the basic concept of discoverability in this Magic Bakery metaphor.

The more work you have out for sale, the more readers can discover all of your work.

Other Doors?

There are hundreds and hundreds of ways to get readers through one of your doors. Again, your Magic Bakery must have product, be clean, and well lit, meaning people can see what flavor of magic pie they want to try.

An example of one great way is to sell a short story to a magazine or anthology. The door is your story in that book or magazine, which will be different when you publish the story out wide later on.

For example, you sell a story to *Asimov's* and it is printed in their magazine. They get to about a hundred thousand readers through their varied means. That door is now open into your bakery because readers there can enjoy your story and follow your name through the door into your other work.

Bundles are another great door that opens and closes. For example, as I write this, I have novels in two great bundles. Now both novels are out there wide in electronic and paper. But for three weeks, each novel in each bundle will have a new door that readers can follow to my Magic Bakery and all my other work.

There are many, many other ways. From Bookbub to Facebook promotions to Amazon ads to giving a story away on your blog every week and so on. So, so many ways and more being created every day.

But the basic premise is that any time you can set up a way for readers to find one of your stories, it creates a door into your bakery and all your other work.

Create Doors By Creating More Product

One of the most common questions I get is about collections. The question is always in a form like this: "If I have five of my short stories in a collection, should I also publish them stand-alone?"

My answer is always yes, of course. A collection is one door times all the places you have it for sale. For sake of the math, say 1 x 12 equals 12 doors.

If you put up the stories as stand-alone stories as well, you have created 60 more doors. So with stories in a collection and stand-alone, you would have at least 72 doors into your bakery.

That many more chances that a reader can discover your Magic Bakery and come in and sample more.

Take those 30 stories I wrote in April of 2017. I created 30 magic pies. Let's count the doors into my Magic Bakery I got from that month of having fun writing short fiction.

Each story will be published stand-alone. 30 x 12 = 360 doors.

Each will be put into a *Smith's Monthly* volume. About 8 volumes. 8 x 12 = 96 doors.

Each will be put in a five-story collection at some point. 6 collections. 6 x 12 = 72 doors.

So from writing 30 stories in 30 days and getting them out wide and in various forms, I created about 528 new entrance doors into my Magic Bakery. And who knows what the future of those 30 stories holds for even more doors.

That's why productivity is king in this new world. The more magic pies, the more doors into your bakery.

Now For Some Real Magic

The magic pie (your story) never leaves your bakery. Yet at the same time, that story exists out in all those places for readers to sample and find the door back to where that magic pie lives and all your other work lives.

Through the magic of copyright, your magic pie can be on the shelf in your store, completely in your control, while also being available for someone to license and read in electronic form all over the world.

So that is pretty nifty magic all by itself. It is the basis for the modern Magic Bakery.

But there is more. The magic of paper copies.

A paper copy of your book gets printed and sold. One reader found the door to your work. All great.

But that paper copy, not the place it was sold, but the paper copy itself, remains a door to your store as well.

How is that?

Say the book was read and then was donated to a library and sold there. So now that paper copy opened the door to your bakery for another reader.

This can't happen with electronic licenses. One sale, one customer. But not paper.

Say the book ends up in a used bookstore, the most magical place of all for opening doors to writer's Magic Bakeries. And someone finds it, takes it home, likes it and opens a door into your bakery.

Then trades the book back in or gives it to a library or to a friend.

So you have your work for sale on Amazon and a few other places in paper. Each place is a door to your bakery times the number of books you have in print.

But watch the number of sales each month in print, because each sale is a potential new door into your work for a reader or numbers of new readers at some point.

This concept has always been around, just never talked much about in the old traditional days. Writers back then only had one door and that was to sell the story to a publisher. And Magic Bakeries are pretty much non-existent when you sell all rights to traditional publishers.

But now paper copies can be a massive tool in bringing in loyal customers to your Magic Bakery because every paper book sold becomes a possible number of future doors.

The New World of Discoverability (I mean doors)

The thinking is simple: The more product you have in your Magic Bakery, the more possible doors there are out there for someone to find your work.

But you can see why I have always shouted about the silliness of being exclusive anywhere. It limits your doors into your bakery. It really is that simple.

And the more doors you have, the more people can find your Magic Bakery with all your work sitting gleaming on the shelves.

And the more product in your place, the more doors and the more readers will shop around when they do find you.

So above I said I have about 3,600 doors plus into my bakery. That number was based on just electronic license.

But hundreds of my books are in print and selling and each time one books sells,

I know for a fact that one copy that sold might be a future door to a brand new customer.

And that's why sometimes my Magic Bakery gets real crowded with customers. And for any shop owner, that is a fun thing to see.

CHAPTER NINE

Success and the Future

NOW THERE ARE two words that almost every writer I have met can't fathom or even see when it comes to their own writing and business.

Now granted, some writers give those two words lip service, and in different workshops Kris and I work at getting writers to think ahead. It feels like walking into a brick wall.

Success and future planning when it comes to writing and a publishing business are just not possible for almost every writer to fathom.

And honestly, I understand that. My goal, for a very long time, was to make a living at my writing. I had NO concept what that meant other than the basics of "paying my bills" with my writing income that month.

Notice the thought is making a living, not a career. A living can happen for a year. And a ton of writers in this modern world of indie publishing can make a living for a year or two, as long as the hot-new-trend they stumbled into continues.

You see this a great deal in the writers in Kindle Select. (And three years from the time I write this writers will be asking me "What was Kindle Select?") This book of blog posts will far, far outlast that blip in the publishing history.

These writers give no thought at all to building a career.

Let me give a quick definition that I use. "Making a Living" is a very short-term goal. "Building a Career" is the ability to make a living every year, year-after-year, over decades.

Everything I teach and everything in this book is aimed at helping writers build careers. If you want the most recent fad, go have fun. Bank the money is my suggestion.

So now, for this chapter, I am going to talk mostly about success.

Selling to Traditional Publishing

Got to deal with this first because to many beginning writers, simply selling to a major publisher is a success.

The sad writers who do this in 2017 (as I write this) are not giving one thought to the future or long-term career building. They are selling all rights to their books for a few thousand dollars and the pat on their heads that tells them that some English major in an office in New York really likes them.

Then for a short time a year or two later their books will be published over-priced, restricted in distribution, and with a great sense of "Is that all there is?"

Soon the book will be pushed to the back and forgotten, just an IP valuation on a corporate balance sheet. But wow is their family proud of them, but wonder why they are still working their day jobs.

To these writers success is measured by a sale to a single editor. That's it.

That's their definition of success. Sort of sad, huh?

And by signing the contract they make their future with those books very simple. They no longer own the books, so those books have no future.

Reality of Numbers

Publishing is a very large industry. Very large. And if you know how to manage your magic pies correctly, your work in publishing can extend into many other areas as well. Movies, television, games, to name just some obvious ones.

But writers tend to be focused on how to make an extra sale here, or give something away there, to gain more imaginary numbers on a mailing list. These writers make no plans and have no concept at all of what might happen when it comes to real success and real money.

One question we do in both the online monthly business class and a variation of it in the Strengths Business workshop, is what would happen if you knew suddenly that in three months 100,000 dollars would hit your account.

The answers are head-shaking because it is clear no writer we have asked that question to has thought ahead to that kind of small success. (And yes, that is a small success in publishing.)

And if you are thinking you would take that small success, I sure understand. But that also illustrates the problem. Your vision, your ability to see a future and real success, is very limited.

A good attorney friend of mine once said that he envied me with my job. He went to work, made great money, and then went home. All the money he could make in a day he made. To keep making money he had to go back to work the next day. But when I got up and went to writing, every day I had a chance of hitting a home run and making millions.

And sometimes that possibility was with a novel I wrote years before.

He saw the publishing profession so much better than most writers.

Sadly, there is nothing I can say to most here in this chapter to convince most anyone. Think about it. Even those who do make the huge money are always called "lucky" or "outliers" by those who can't imagine doing it themselves.

There is a vested interest in writers as a class to not think about real success or the future.

So What Do You Do to Get Ready for Success?

First, never sell your entire magic pie. For any reason to anyone.

Keep that magic pie, that copyright, firmly planted in your bakery.

That is the basic center of everything. Then your pie, as the future unfolds, can earn you money.

What else can you do?

—Start studying writers who are successful in careers. Not those flash writers chasing the most recent trend. Study

writers who have been writing and selling and in a career in one form or another for decades. There are a lot of us.

—Start understanding business and money. Your Magic Bakery is a business. Start understanding things like cash streams, corporations, tax protections, and so on. For example, that 100,000 you get in suddenly. If you understand what I just said, you will keep it all. If you don't, you will pay over half of it to governments.

—Start learning how stories and novels get outside of publishing. What do you need to do? Learn that.

—Get your work into every market you can around the world and let it build. And keep writing what you love.

—Learn all the ways you can divide up your magic pies.

—Then be patient. You can't learn any of the above overnight, or even in a year.

You are a writer. Write the next book, the next story, the next blog post as I am doing here.

Then, as I am doing here, after you are finished, see how many ways you can turn slices of the pie you just created into cash streams.

Next chapter will be about thinking about the future. You know, that place beyond Christmas.

CHAPTER TEN

Beyond Next Year

AS I SAID LAST chapter, it has been my observation that most writers never look more than a year out, if that. And that lack of being able to see five years and ten years and 50 years into the future causes all sorts of really bad decisions.

Now, I wish I could say I had been an exception to this in my first few decades or so in publishing. Nope. Kris was a bunch better at looking long term and making decisions based on that vision. But I wasn't.

And wow did I make some bone-headed mistakes because of that lack of vision. So now here I am trying to maybe help one or two people expand into the future their plans and hopes and focus.

The Magic Bakery

It is the future that really is important in a Magic Bakery. Let me try to explain why in just a couple simple points.

—Your copyright, your magic pie, will last and stay fresh for 70 years past your death (In the US, 50 years in other countries). At that 70 year mark your heirs will lose control over it, but that does not mean they still can't make money from it for another 70 years or longer.

—You have no idea what technology will be coming in the next century. No clue. (New ways to cut your magic pie.)

(Example: I wrote one of the very first electronic books Pocket Books ever published. The year was 2000 and trust me, even with electronic books being sort of in existence for a decade or more before that, I thought it stupid. Shows what I knew. Again, in those years I wasn't the best at seeing the future.)

—If you structure the business of your bakery correctly (a coming chapter), your business will not only make you a lot of money in your lifetime, but also survive you and thrive. But the business has to be set up for the future.

So Many Ways to Fail

Those three points above seem very simple and obvious, don't they? But wow can you fail in so many ways when you stand in your Magic Bakery, surrounded by all your magic pies, and have no sense of tomorrow.

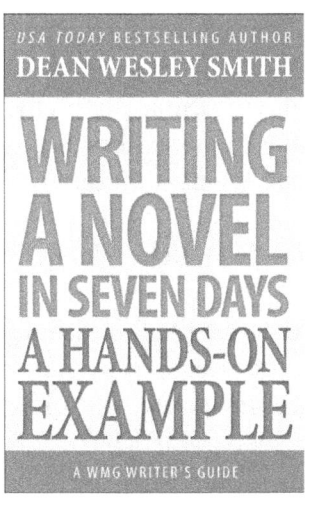

Let me give you three major failure points.

—Sell your book to a major traditional publisher (or movie producer) for all rights for the term of the copyright. Pie vanishes from your bakery. Writers who do this give zero thought to the future of their business at all. To them their book has no value beyond the tiny pat on the head traditional publishers give them and a little bit of money. Or hope for a movie that won't get made.

—You don't learn business and sales, so your store sits there with few customers and eventually you drift away to do something else. Your pies never mold or grow old, but dust covers the shelves and paint peels off the front of your store and no one goes in. (This happens to 80-90% of all fiction writers, sadly.)

You all know this kind of thing. Your store becomes a "whatever-happened-to?" store. We have all walked down a mall, seen an empty spot and asked "Whatever happened to that place?" Imagine that was where your Magic Bakery was at and you get the sad idea of what happens when you quit.

—You don't understand how Intellectual Property (IP) works, so you make no preparation for the day something happens to you. So those 70 years plus that your Magic Bakery could remain open and flourishing and making your family or some charity money vanish when they dump your body in the ground.

All three of those major failure points are from lack of being able to deal with the future.

A Ticking Time Bomb

Remember a few chapters back I mentioned the new world of IP Valuation? Not your issue, right? Your stories only make a few hundred so they can't be worth much. Right?

Again, no thought to any future. Courts and estate probate judges are understanding IP valuation and are starting to apply different forms of evaluation. If you are making a nice bit of money from your stories and you have not set up the right structure to move your IP to your heirs, they could get hit with a tax bill upon your death that could destroy everything. Wouldn't that be a nice gift to leave your family?

Easily fixed if you think about the future at all. But alas, most writers don't.

And that leads to the next problem—

What Is Your Magic Bakery Worth?

Most newer writers and all traditionally published writers would say nothing. And the reason for that is that there are no pies on the shelves. The bakery is mostly empty.

USA TODAY BESTSELLING AUTHOR
DEAN WESLEY SMITH
KILLING
THE TOP 10
Sacred Cows
OF PUBLISHING
A WMG WRITER'S GUIDE

More WMG Writers' Guides
from all your favorite booksellers
in trade paper and electronic editions.

Even if there were magic pies on those shelves, most writers would still say it wasn't worth much at all. Why? Because they can't see past a year or so.

Now I understand that moving forward, IP needs freshening at times to remain attractive to the current buyer. Not going to talk about that ongoing task. I know it all too well. So for this, I will assume you do that work, or have it done, or your estate will do it.

So if you can imagine that as a possibility, what might your bakery be worth?

For what amount would I sell all rights to all 300 of my magic pies, plus the bakery itself? What kind of future income do my 300 plus magic pies have possible?

And in three years that number will be past 400, and so on, not counting all the IP that will return to me under the 35 year rule starting in 2026.

Impossible to calculate. But fun to look at when you realize you really are creating something of value, even though it only sells five copies a year. It still has value.

Heinlein's Rule #2 states simply: Finish what you write.

When you finish a story, you have added value to your Magic Bakery. It really is that simple.

How To Learn To Think Forward

Sure, work to make money now. Work to sell your stuff now. But all the while, keep these basic things in mind.

—Never allow your IP to leave your bakery. You license slices, nothing more. For only the term needed and when the term is up that slice will magically appear back in your pie.

—When discouraged, thinking of shutting the doors for good, do an inventory of your existing IP. Then try to put a value on it, keeping in mind your lifetime and 70 years beyond. Imagine two or three things being made into movies, imagine others being games, still others being part of some unknown tech. Then write the next story or book and add even more value.

—Learn Business. Tons of great books for small businesses out there. Understand what a good year of growth might be. That will help with perspective instead of always listening to the latest fad from the latest hot guru of marketing and thinking you are not doing enough.

—Learn Estates. It will help you if you figure out a way to help your favorite family and/or charity with your business if you can get it large enough. In other words, write your fun stories for a larger purpose in the future.

—Make It a Challenge. You want to have the best bakery. The most successful. The larger, the nicer your bakery is, the more customers you will get, the more sales, the more value. But building the best bakery takes time. Growing any business takes time. Make it a challenge. Not something to be afraid of, but something to have fun with.

Summary

A wonderful thing about our Magic Bakeries: They really are magical.

Copyright is an amazing ingredient in our pies that allows us to build and run these wonderful places full of diverse products. And magically attract customers from all over the world.

Our magic pies can be enjoyed as a book, a movie, an audio file, in tons of different languages, and who knows what else is coming in the future. All without ever leaving our bakery.

Copyright also allows us the time to build these magical places.

You just have to know that the future is out there and first accept it, then plan for it.

CHAPTER ELEVEN

Maintenance

THIS BOOK, AT its heart, has been about the business of fiction. And selling fiction. And the copyright associated with fiction.

Fact: So many writers ignore copyright and eventually go away. Long-term writers know copyright and know how to get every bit of money we can from copyright. That might be the most important element to why a long-term writer is a long-term writer and not a "what-ever-happened-to" writer.

Fact: So many writers equate the hours it took to write something with the value of the story. A short story can't have much value because it only took four hours to write it. That is the thinking. I hear that all the time with writers afraid to charge a fair value for their short stories. Head-shaking.

And those two "facts" cause extreme problems, both large and small. And where those two facts come into play the most is in the long-term maintenance of copyright.

How I Learned Value

Early on as a writer, I too equated the value of the time spent with the value of the story. Now understand, I considered

myself expensive. I would never sell a story for under 5 cents per word and almost never did a media book for less than $20,000. Often a lot more and ghost novels even more than that.

And I could spend hours writing every day, so I was considered fast. And thus it didn't take me much time at all to earn that advance on a novel or the sale money from a short story. So in my head I had set some value for my work at the amount I could get out of it and that was related to the time I spent writing it.

One simple story fairly early in my career quickly proved to me how stupid that very short-sighted thinking was. The story was called "In the Shade of the Slowboat Man." I wrote it in under three hours while sitting facing Nina Kiriki Hoffman in a living room at a writer's retreat. It was one of three short stories I did in that day or so.

It was for a vampire anthology, but the editor bounced it because it was too "nice" for his anthology. So I was about to toss it in a drawer when Kris forced me to send it to Ed Ferman at F&SF and he bought it. And then it was on the final Nebula ballot that year and in the Nebula Awards Anthology as well. Cool. I made a little more than I expected from it. But my worldview as to value and time was still intact.

Until I got an offer for a radio play for the short story and they hired Kris to write the script. And suddenly that three-hour short story made us another $10,000 and was turned into a really great radio play.

And then the story got picked up for a number of reprint places and optioned once for a movie and I made money on all that. (I still think it would make a great movie.)

And then I ended up reprinting it in Smith's Monthly and also putting it up as a stand-alone for $2.99 in electronic and $4.99 in paper and it sells regularly every year for years now.

Three hours. One simple short story. Twenty-plus years after I wrote the short story, it is still earning me money, more money every year than I expected to get from it at first.

That was the first story that finally got me realizing the long-term value of copyright. I have other short stories now that I have made more money on. "Jukebox Gifts" as an example.

Those magic pies are very popular with the customers of my Magic Bakery.

Maintenance of the Magic Bakery

As I said last chapter, magic pies do not spoil.

But sadly, they can be forgotten. And often are.

Now at the ten-year mark of indie publishing, there are statistics coming out now about the large percentage of stories and books that sell no copies in a year. (This was always the case before, but no one talked about that.)

Think of all the billions of stories and novels now available to readers as a giant ocean. In this new world, the stories that sell are the ones on the surface of the giant ocean of fiction available to readers.

The ones that don't sell are far, far below the surface, down in the dark, impossible to find or sell.

Now when I started into indie publishing, I had over a hundred published traditional novels, over 60 of which were under this name. And everyone thought that I was lucky. Used to make me very angry when someone would say that

because I knew the truth. I wasn't lucky. I considered someone starting fresh lucky. I had a massive wall in front of me to climb over.

When you clicked on my name on Amazon back then, all you saw was Star Trek, Men in Black, gaming novels and so on. Books I had been paid for and didn't make another dime on and did not own the magic pie.

So when I started I put up in fairly quick order over 50 of my own short stories. When you clicked on Amazon, my highest short story was nine pages deep in the list of 50 plus pages of my novels and stories at that point.

Deep is the operative word there. My stories were way, way deep under the surface and impossible to see. Driven to the depths by my success in traditional publishing.

So I knew I only had one choice if I was going to make a career under this name in this modern world. I had to churn the surface of the ocean of books and do a lot of product and basically overwhelm

the system. And I did. Not with any promotion tricks, but with simple production.

And it took me years.

Do those early stories I put up now sell? Very few of them, because I have not spent the time and energy to dive to get them and bring them back to the surface. (I will. All planned, actually.)

They are magic pies, sitting on my shelves in my bakery, but I have turned the lights off on that corner of the bakery. No one can see the pies, so they don't buy any of them.

So maintenance of the inventory of the bakery is critical.

And difficult.

A Sample of Maintenance

Kris has figured out a way to keep the older stories and novels from sitting in a corner with the lights off. For the short stories, she puts up a free short story on her blog every week. She has been doing this for years and years.

The story is still for sale on all the wide markets, of course. Only free on her blog.

And when she puts the story up for free, often WMG puts a new cover on it if it is an older story, we redo the blurb, and so on. In other words, she brushes off the dust from the magic pie and puts a spotlight over the pie and makes it a weekly special in her bakery.

And the story not only is free, but people buy it that week and often the story will keep on selling at a decent pace for some time to come.

Value for Decades

Magic pies can last a very long time if you are smart with contracts and don't let the entire pie leave your bakery. The pies can last for at least 50 or 70 years past your death (depending on your country) and even after that they will still have value.

But they will not have much value if you do not maintain them.

Magic Bakeries are like any other retail store. The inventory must be kept clean, the lights on for customers to see the product, and the door unlocked for anyone to enter from anywhere in the world.

There must also be someone to run the business and keep the bills paid, even after you die.

But more than anything else, the inventory must be moved around at times, displays changed, standard sales techniques used.

And the value of each pie in your bakery can't be determined by either the year you created the pie or the time it took to create. Your customers will not care about any of that.

You, the owner of the Magic Bakery must believe in every pie. And if the lights over a pie start to flicker, change the bulb.

In Summary

I'm surprised, but the Magic Bakery, as a metaphor for copyright and the fiction writing business, does not seem to stretch too far in any area. When I started this, I thought it would.

Some basics I hope you got from this book in one metaphor or another.

—Writers need to learn to think like real businesses.

—Writers need to learn to think like retail and wholesale businesses.

—Writers need to learn copyright so they understand the ingredients of each pie they are creating and how the magic works.

—And writers, lastly, need to give value to their own work. Both as it is created, the year after it was created, and a hundred years after it was created.

The ocean full of reading will not be decreasing. So it is up to each writer to keep their stories near the surface and readers and buyers coming into their Magic Bakeries.

Now this book, this magic pie will take its rightful place in my bakery. I hope you enjoyed it as much as I did writing it.

And if you did, I hope you will try another pie. After all, magic pies are not fattening.

EPILOGUE

A Comment Reminded Me
of Something

AS I SAID, I did this book in a series of blogs on my website. And there were some great comments along the way. One brought up this last short chapter.

I used to wonder what rights I could sell to my fiction. What exactly those rights were all called. I thought for the longest time there were rules and I just couldn't find the rules or the secret door to go through to discover where those rules were posted.

I think all of us feel that way early on because we don't understand the true nature of copyright when we start writing. In fact, most writers, even though they will spend years writing, don't have a clue what they are trying to sell or license. And won't spend one minute trying to learn it.

Let alone learn the real nature of copyright, the deep down nature of it. That takes time to really understand.

So the truth? There is no magic list of what you can and can't sell in your copyright. Or what the names are of those magical things you slice out of your copyright pie.

And there are certainly no rules.
NONE.
ZERO. ZIP. ZILCH.

It took me some time to realize that as well.

I wanted to know what exactly First Serial Rights meant and First Anthology Rights, or Non-exclusive Anthology Rights and so on and so on, not realizing those are just made-up terms for contracts to help two parties define exactly what is needed.

And the reason those terms are used regularly, if you actually look at the terms, is because they clearly define a way to slice a copyright pie.

In essence, what I am trying to say is this: To describe the piece of your copyright pie you are licensing to another person in a contract, you can call it anything the two of you agree to that will be clear as to what is being licensed.

Now I had a comment wishing I had put more "meat" in my Magic Bakery book. The person had hoped I would define all that stuff. Even if I had tried, I would be wrong for the very next contract you saw.

How can I define terms, put meat, as the comment said, in an article when the very question shows a lack of knowledge of copyright in contracts?

There is no meat past you learning copyright and understanding that you are free to define the slice of your pie in any way you see fit. As long as you and the person on the other side of the contract agree to the definition or name you put on it.

The Magic Bakery Book was an attempt at helping with some basic understanding of copyright and business in this new world of publishing. I put all the "meat" I could in it and still keep it at a basic level.

As a young writer, not understanding copyright, I would have been disappointed as well that the book didn't give the secret handshake and the location of where all those terms were hidden.

Ahh, well. I knew the danger of trying to do a book on copyright in a world where writers are flat determined to not learn it.

So let me start the list of "meat" for those of you still looking for the sacred scroll of terms locked in that hidden vault in a Chicago basement. Then maybe you will understand the vault really is empty.

Example

Take your most recent magic pie off the shelf and get out a sharp magic knife. Then cut out a very, very thin slice to license and in the contract for that slice you can call that license "First North American Refrigerator Magnet Rights."

You can and should reserve "First English Refrigerator Magnet Rights" in the contract because you never know about those companies in other parts of the world. (A different slice.)

Also hold back all "Refrigerator Magnet Translation Rights." (Yet another slice.)

And make sure you are clear in your terms in your contract that the right does not include "First North American Button Rights." (Yet another slice.)

And make sure you say that all other rights are reserved to the author so nothing leaves your magic pie by accident.

Those are all real rights, folks, and if you can't figure out what they are, just slowly say aloud the name of the slice. The words describe the slice of the pie you are licensing.

It really is that simple.

As I said numbers of times in different chapters, every pie can be sliced into thousands of slices, limited only by your imagination on how to limit a right and your understanding of the basic nature of copyright.

As one reader said, and gave me permission to repeat, there is a simple formula for all of this.

The DJ Formula—

Time position + territory + language + usage = rights

Time Position = First, Second, Third, etc.

Territory = hemisphere, country, state, moon, Mars, etc.

Language = English, French, Spanish, etc.

Usage = anything that displays text, images, such as radio, movies, books, plays, comics, buttons, tea towels, etc.

Use that formula anytime you are trying to figure out how to slice your magic pie. It will do wonders to help you through any confusion you might have.

Hope that helps some with adding "meat" into the book. Magic Meat I suppose.

And finally, the metaphor stretched too far and broke.

~

Now Available
from all your favorite booksellers
in trade paper and electronic editions.

USA TODAY BESTSELLING AUTHOR
DEAN WESLEY SMITH

HEINLEIN'S
RULES

FIVE SIMPLE
BUSINESS RULES
FOR WRITING

A WMG WRITER'S GUIDE

DEAN WESLEY SMITH

THE LAST SHORT PUTT OF A FEARFUL MAN

Golf often imitates life. For Todd Bakersfield, golf became life.

One simple par five. Five simple days in a week.

When golf imitates life, playing safe, keeping it in play never seems to work.

A golf story of a fearful man and a final shot for redemption.

THE LAST SHORT PUTT
OF A FEARFUL MAN

Monday

The eighteenth hole stretched out in front of him like a gentle left turn on an interstate.

Dark blue water, roughed by the breeze into small waves, lapped at the edge of the mowed grass along the entire left side, ending five hundred and twenty yards away in front of the green.

Par five.

Todd Bakersfield stood on the tee, driver in hand, staring out over the water at the wide expanse of green fairway calling for his shot.

So easy.

Just ignore the water. But his mind wouldn't let him take out the image of that massive blue death trap.

Par the hole, a simple five, and he would win. Hit it in the water and he wouldn't have a chance.

He glanced down at his teed-up ball, then back out at the fairway. He hadn't beaten his long-time golfing buddies, Peter and Stan in years. Yet now, today of all days, all he had to do was par the last hole.

But if he hit his drive into the water, it wouldn't happen.

Not today, maybe not ever.

He stood over the ball, trying to not to think about the water as Monday drifted back into focus.

Monday… The start of the worst five days of his life.

ONE

HIS BOSS'S OFFICE had been hot. And the leather chair facing Robin McCarthey's desk was, for the first time, uncomfortable.

As a section chief in research, Todd had sat in that chair a hundred times over the past ten years and not once had it been as uncomfortable.

And not once had Robin's office been that hot and sticky.

"Not looking good, is it?" Todd had asked, trying to smile.

Robin shook his head. "Not for any of us, I'm afraid."

Todd couldn't get the twisting out of his stomach.

Robin shook his head and sat back. "We were bought out this morning. Two hours ago. I'd say they'll close this entire building by the end of the year. Six months at most. Wouldn't make sense for them to keep up duplicate services any longer than that."

Todd wasn't surprised at all. The threatened corporate take-over had been rumored for a month. He worried about his people, the twelve who had looked to him for answers every day.

Just as he was looking to Robin right now.

Impossible situation. There were no answers.

Todd knew it.

Robin knew it.

"I'm sure everyone will get some options, possibly transfer," Robin said. "Or at the least good severance packages. We'll know later in the week would be my guess. But for now, we just keep doing our jobs."

Todd had nodded, agreed.

Keep it in play.

He stood on the tee, remembering he had thought that on Monday.

He took a breath.

Keep it in play.

His drive went right, bouncing along the right side of the fairway, farther from the green, but away from the instant death of the water on the left side.

Keep it in play, look at the next shot.

Tuesday

The wind was in his face and the water on the left of the now narrow strip of green still loomed like a giant monster ready to snap anything that got close.

He looked down the right.

Only problem there was some shallow rough and a few small trees. It would leave a longer shot into the green, but that would be a small price to pay for staying out of the water.

TWO

TWO OF HIS best people gave him notice and quit, coming in and cleaning out their desks. They already had other jobs lined up and were just cutting and moving instead of waiting.

Todd didn't blame them. Everyone else mostly stood and talked and nothing got done really, except they got through Tuesday.

They advanced the calendar and nothing more.

His second shot bounced along the right edge of the fairway, far, far from any trouble.

He advanced the ball and got through the second shot.

Wednesday

Now the wind, a short time before only a slight breeze, seemed like a gale directly in his face, dropping the temperature and making his eyes water. At the moment he wished he'd brought a jacket, even though he knew he wouldn't put it on this close to the end of the round.

The blue devil-water guarded the front left of the big green while the pin hid on the back right, seemingly impossible to reach up on a fortress-like mound.

All he needed was no disaster.

A simple short iron to the center of the green, two putts to win for the first time in years and years.

He knew exactly what to do.

THREE

ROBIN HAD CALLED him in early Wednesday morning and tossed a packet across the desk at him.

Todd had been around Robin far, far too long. He knew without asking that what was in that packet was bad news.

Todd went to pick it up as Robin stood and turned away, staring out his window at nothing but the half-empty parking lot.

"We're done at the end of the week," Robin said. "They figure it's better to do everything quick and move on."

"This week?" Todd asked, not really believing what he had heard.

"This week," Robin said, his back to Todd. "We all get two month's severance as a gesture of good faith."

It sounded as if he spat the word "faith."

Todd dropped down into the soft leather chair facing his boss's desk and held the packet in his hands, actually afraid to open it and see in writing what Robin had told him.

"Well," Todd said, finally, "at least now I'll have time to work on my putting."

Robin didn't laugh.

There was no reason to laugh.

Thursday

The wind held his third shot in the air for what seemed like an eternity before dropping it on the front of the green. He was still a long ways from the pin, but at least he had avoided the water.

That much was a victory.

Now two putts and he'd be done.

Or at least he hoped he would be.

Todd rubbed the sweat off the inside of his right hand and studied the seemingly mile-long putt.

Just as in his job, he had played this hole safe. He had advanced the ball and nothing more.

But at the moment he knew exactly what to do.

He had to get the ball close to the hole.

He walked the length of the long putt three times, studying it from all sides, all the time trying to make his nerves calm down.

Around him the day had turned almost frigid, with the wind picking up.

He tried to ignore the wind and the cold and to study what was in front of him. He didn't have to make the putt. He only had to get it so close that he wouldn't miss the next one.

Just get it close.

FOUR

ALMOST EVERYONE WORK-ING for him came in and cleaned out their desks on Thursday.

They were all going to take sick days Friday, since none of them could see a reason to come in to work. Their work was now worthless.

Todd didn't blame them.

He would have been doing the same thing if he hadn't been their boss. But for some reason he felt the need to stay to the bitter end.

At exactly five he left.

Tomorrow he would clean out his desk.

When his wife Maggie had died fifteen years ago, golf and his job had become the focus of his life. At night he watched the Golf Channel, practiced evenings on the driving range, and played Saturday and Sunday.

But Saturday against the guys was always the important day.

He knew that if he kept practicing, working on his game, studying, some day he would beat them. He just knew it.

Maybe that someday was today.

What would they do if he did?

What would he do?

Robin came into his department and looked around.

"Where did everyone go?"

"They all left," Todd said, "not even waiting, or caring to see what the company offered them."

Robin nodded. "I was just told the company is dumping everything on the new department and I'm supposed to go along for a few weeks and help them get it all straightened out."

"You're kidding, right?" Todd asked.

Robin just shook his head and turned and left.

One nice thing had happened that day. All the people who had worked for Todd had said how much they liked him. The women gave him a hug, the men a solid handshake.

And then they were gone.

All his people.

And he was alone.

Friday

He hit the putt a little too timidly and the slight hill between him and the hole killed the ball's speed, turning it away from the hole.

It stopped two feet short of the hole.

He had never given the birdie putt a chance to even go in the hole.

Now he had to make a two-foot putt for a par and a win.

In all the years of Saturday mornings, he had never won.

Maybe today, of all days, after one of the worst weeks in his life, he would win for the first time.

Two feet of smooth grass between his ball and the hole.

Two short feet.

Yet the more he studied the putt, the more confused, the more afraid he became.

The wind was now blowing around him so hard, it seemed to shake the ball, wanting to send it down off the green and into the lake.

Somehow it stayed there, perched, waiting for him to work up his courage.

FIVE

HE HAD WAITED most of Friday, sitting at his desk in an empty office, pretending to fill a few boxes with his things.

This job had been a part of his life for as long as he could remember. Maggie had said he was good at it, and now he was packing her picture. He was nothing more than a discarded employee, lost in the shuffle of corporate mergers.

He stared at the picture of his beautiful wife, now frozen forever at forty. He knew he wasn't being honest with himself. It wasn't the company that had thrown away his life. He had, by not acting, by staying in one place too long, by not going out and taking chances.

Now he had forgotten how to take chances.

He'd had his job, his house, and his golf.

Now he only had his house and his golf.

At exactly five, he walked out of the office for the last time, got into his car and headed for the driving range.

As he always did on Friday evening he bought a large bucket of balls. It would take him one hour to hit all the balls.

One hour later, the last shot he hit on the driving range was a driver.

He hit it squarely and for the first time all day, he smiled as it bounced directly over the two hundred-yard sign.

On the way home to his empty house, a drunk driver in a large truck ran through a red light and hit him squarely in the driver's side of his five-year-old sedan.

The crash sprung the trunk of his car and scattered his golf clubs down the street like broken dreams.

Saturday

Todd stood on the green, braced himself against the strong winds, then with one last glance at the hole, he hit the ball.

The last two-foot putt caught the edge of the cup and spun out.

He'd had a chance to win and had blown it.

He had felt exactly the same way all week, spending most of the time just wondering how things had gone so wrong.

Not taking any chances, playing it safe.

Just as he had done his entire life.

Playing it safe and losing.

As he watched, the ball spun away from the hole and picked up speed, pushed by the wind and the slope.

A moment later the ball bounced over the edge of the green and rolled down the slope into the cold, wind-whipped water.

The water he had been so afraid of. The water he had played away from to be safe.

He stared at the water for a moment, the putter clutched in his hand, not really believing what had happened.

Then he turned and looked back at the hole he had just played.

The life he had just lived.

An hour after they took his body to the morgue, a young policeman picked up Todd's golf clubs and tossed them into the trunk of Todd's wrecked car to be scrapped with everything else from Todd's safe life.

USA *Today* Bestselling Writer

DEAN WESLEY
SMITH

TOMBSTONE CANYON
A Thunder Mountain Story

Looking for a home in the West, Dan Gray finds a hidden canyon a few years before the gold boom of Roosevelt, Idaho.

Just up the valley from Roosevelt, Dan's hidden canyon offers a place to build in safety and with privacy.

A story of a wandering man finding a home.

And peace at the same time.

Author's Note:

I published Tombstone Canyon: A Thunder Mountain Novel *in* Smith's Monthly #41. *This story by the same name started that novel. And parts of it, in altered fashion, exist in the book.*

TOMBSTONE CANYON:
The Short Story
A Thunder Mountain Story

ONE

Monumental Creek
Central Idaho
July, 1899

DAN GRAY, FORMERLY of Kansas City, now living pretty much everywhere in the West, let his horse lead him at its own pace up a game trail along a stream called Monumental Creek on a map. The stream looked like it might have some nice trout in it and maybe tonight after he made camp he would see what he could catch for dinner.

Nothing beat the taste of fresh, pan-fried trout in the evening.

Tall stands of mountain pine were around him, broken by meadows of knee-high grass.

Above the trees, the towering mountains still had some snow on the tallest peaks even though it was July. But down in the deep valley where he was, especially for the hours the sun got to the bottom of the valley, the air was warm, so warm he had taken off his top coat a few miles back and rode only in his rolled-up shirt sleeves. He had stopped a few times to splash cold snowmelt stream water on his face and neck and over his head.

He kept a wet bandana covering his neck under his cowboy hat and at the moment it was about dried out.

Looking at him, a person would think Dan Gray was just another broke mountain man, working to eke out some food and find a little color in the streams to buy supplies when he needed them. With his dark beard and longish dark hair, he looked older than his thirty-two years.

Actually, Dan Gray was a stupidly wealthy cattleman. He had gotten bored, very bored with the cattle business that had made him so rich. He had needed something different and west, beyond the Rockies, called to him like a lost lover. And he had been right, it was just about as different as it got from Kansas City, especially in the late 1890s.

So without his business partner knowing, he had transferred enough money into a dozen western banks along the coast to be rich the rest of his life, told his partner the business was his to do with as he pleased, signed it all over, mounted up and headed out.

In two winters and two summers now, he had kept moving and never regretted for a moment his decision. He had no idea what he was looking for, but he believed he would know it when he found it.

He knew deep down what he was looking for more than anything was just a place to live, a place to claim as his own and build a home.

And he wanted to build it himself, no matter how long it took.

Ahead the steep-walled canyon widened slightly into a small meadow and Dan got off the horse and let it graze as

Former PGA Golf Professional and USA Today *bestselling writer Dean Wesley Smith walks you step-by-step, club-by-club from your car to the first tee and beyond in a laugh-out-loud style that not only teaches, but entertains.*

A perfect gift for the golfer in your family.

Now Available
from all your favorite booksellers in trade paper and electronic editions.

he went to splash more water on his face and get his bandana wet again.

It was at that point he saw the canyon through the trees, or at least thought he saw the canyon.

Over the years in the cattle business, a cowboy got used to losing cattle up small side canyons, often canyons hidden from view of those in the main canyon.

A canyon like that would show up face-on as nothing more than what looked like a crack in a rock wall. But if you went up to the wall, you could see part of the wall was much father out than the other part, forming a path or corridor that went off from the main canyon at almost a ninety-degree angle.

There were canyons all over the Southwest marked "hidden canyon" on maps if they were near known cattle drive routes. Those hidden canyons could make cattle just seemingly vanish.

In his days on the trails early on, he had checked out more hidden canyons than he wanted to think about.

Dan studied the rock wall across the narrow valley. From where he was, it sure looked like a hidden canyon opening.

He finished filling his canteen with the bitingly cold fresh water, splashed more on his face and neck, then put his soaking-wet bandana on his neck, sending shivers down his spine.

Then he let his horse drink a little before he mounted up and splashed across the stream through the pine trees toward the canyon wall.

There was no trail, not even game trails, so he had to do a little bushwhacking through some brush under the trees.

Less than five minutes later he discovered he had been right.

He was facing the opening to a hidden canyon.

Anyone moving along the stream as he had been doing would never see the entrance unless they got lucky like he had and knew what they were looking for.

The canyon opening was wide enough to get a wagon through with moving just a few loose rocks.

He dismounted and tied up his horse in the shade, then started up the canyon through the rocks. After about a hundred paces, the canyon turned into the hillside, rock cliffs on both sides and a small stream coming down the middle.

He could feel himself getting excited. Really excited.

Then, after another hundred paces, the canyon opened up into what looked to be an almost round meadow, with rock walls on all sides and a waterfall cascading down the far canyon wall.

Stands of pine filled part of the valley floor and a small beaver pond backed up some of the water.

Above him, the towering mountains seemed to guard over the small box-canyon meadow.

Standing there, staring at the beauty, he knew instantly he had found a home.

TWO

Off Monumental Creek
Central Idaho
July, 1899

IT WAS THREE days later, while exploring the canyon to make sure he had every foot of it measured to be recorded down in Boise, that Dan found the old camp.

At the highest part at the back of the canyon away from the entrance, on the upper edge of the trees, on a small rock ledge, were the remains of a trapper's camp.

Bedding and saddlebags still remained, along with some supplies. Clearly the camp had been abandoned here for five or six years. It looked like it had been set up as a winter camp with shelter from the snow under a rock outcropping. He had seen numbers of those in the last few years of riding the west.

But something had happened here. The saddlebags and supplies should not still be here.

To the right of the ledge and down a dozen steps, just in the trees, Dan found the skeleton of a horse, one bullet hole through its head.

At that point Dan knew what had happened.

He kept searching and finally near the camp, under what appeared to be a form of lean-to shelter that had collapsed over the years, Dan found the old trapper, not much more than a skeleton.

He had a gun across his lap and had clearly shot himself in the head as well.

It made Dan sick to his stomach to see it, but it was not the first time he had seen death and not the first time he had seen what the loneliness of the vast western plains and mountains could do to a person.

You had to really love the loneliness or it would crush you like a rockslide.

Clearly this man had been crushed by it.

Dan spent the next day digging the old trapper a grave near the remains of his horse, then he put a large tombstone over the grave. It was a flat rock on which Dan had chiseled the rough words, "Rest in Peace."

He would keep the area clear of brush over the years he planned on living here.

That night, as he sat around his campfire, planning what to do next, he realized that the name of this canyon needed to be Tombstone Canyon, in honor of the trapper who had found it.

A week later, Dan left the hidden canyon and headed back down the main canyon along Monumental Creek. He now had a purpose for the first time in years. He had found a home. Now he had to build a shelter.

It took him three days to get to Boise to register his mining claim in the canyon and purchase the land around the claim inside the rock walls.

He paid with cash and signed all the papers Tombstone Dan, getting a magistrate to make it his legal signature just in case any of the people from his old life were looking for him. He doubted they were, but better safe than sorry.

Dan Gray was officially dead for all intents and purposes, even though he still had a lot of money in banks in the West under that name.

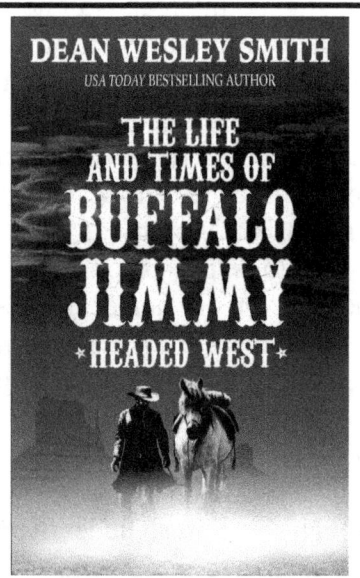

A week later, with three packhorses loaded with supplies and equipment to survive the winter and build the first part of his home, he headed back to Tombstone Canyon.

It had been years since he had felt this excited. He knew he had a hard winter ahead in those high mountains of Idaho.

But he would survive it, he had no doubt.

THREE

Tombstone Canyon
Central Idaho
May, 1900

DAN HAD FINISHED his rough cabin with stone fireplace the previous fall just as the first snow flew. He had also built a shelter for his horses among the trees down by the meadow and stream.

He had decided this first cabin would end up being just storage for him later. He would build his real home on a ledge on the right side of the canyon, with a view of not only the mountains and the rising sun to the east, but of the entrance to the canyon.

Safer that way, even though he never expected anyone to find this canyon. But the trapper had and he had, so someone else might.

As he expected, the winter was long and hard and he kept busy mostly just making sure his horses were doing all right and clearing the snow from around his small cabin doors and one window.

On some days just the hundred-yard hike down to his horses took him an hour through the snow.

But the canyon was small enough to be sheltered from any high winds and the snow didn't get that deep compared to some more open places he had seen.

Then, in May, as he knew it would, the weather cleared.

He had his cabin plan all worked out over the long winter's nights and as soon as he thought it safe, he and his horses headed down the rushing Monumental Creek. This time it took him just over a week to get out, but he made it. Next year he would wait another week or two to start.

In Boise he spent the first full month coming to understand that without some real training, he would never be able to build the cabin he wanted to build on his own.

So he spent a month learning about how to build a solid rock foundation for his cabin, and a solid fireplace. Then he went back into his canyon with supplies and tools enough to get through the summer.

He saw no one and by the time fall rolled around, he had built a large stone foundation for his cabin and a towering rock fireplace and was back in Boise staying at the Boise hotel for the winter.

Two things happened that winter and his life turned once again.

He took lessons in fine home log building from two master craftsmen in town.

And he came to love the game of poker.

He spent his days learning construction, his nights learning poker.

And along the way, he also came to really appreciate the attitude in saloons in the West compared to the cowboy bars back East. Most of the saloon owners kept their bars clean and free of disturbances.

Dan liked that.

And as Dan did with anything he set his mind to, he became good at both construction and poker. He also learned the saloon business, something that he found interesting, far more than the business of cattle.

The following spring, with four pack-horses loaded with supplies, he headed back into his canyon.

He felt more driven, more alive than he had at any time in his past. And the high mountain air only helped that.

By the time the summer was finished, his home was sealed up for the winter. It still wasn't finished inside, but it would withstand the snow and cold on the outside.

And the view from his front porch looking out over the small valley and at the mountains to the east was breathtaking.

He could imagine no better place to be.

He planned on spending one more winter in Boise and working next summer on the interior of his new home before completely moving in. But on the way out, he ran across some placer miners along Monumental Creek.

And they were all finding color.

The winter weather was about to shut them down, but he knew what that meant for next spring. Monumental Creek would be flooded with miners and more than likely towns would spring up.

He didn't worry about anyone finding his canyon. Not only was it naturally protected, but he had it posted and he owned both the land and the claims.

So once he made it back to Boise, he dug into the records and realized that the plat for the town of Roosevelt had already been laid out and parcels were being bought.

Roosevelt would be just two miles below the mouth of his canyon. And for as long as the gold rush existed, he would have company close by.

For some reason, he didn't mind that.

That night, while sitting in a poker game in the wonderful game room of the new Idanha Hotel, he came up with what he needed to do.

The next day he purchased eight of the parcels along the main street of the new town of Roosevelt, spread the length.

Then he first headed to Seattle to draw money out of his account there and then went by ship on down to San Francisco to draw money from a bank he had put money in there as well.

Over the winter in Boise, he put a number of building crews together because they knew him and liked him and he paid well.

The next spring, his building crews descended on the new town of Roosevelt and by the time the summer was over, they had built eight saloons.

And all eight had pianos.

And besides a few of the construction foremen and the official paperwork in Boise, no one in Roosevelt knew he owned the saloons. He had set up a company headquartered in Boise to run them and to build more around the West from the profits coming out of Roosevelt.

Nothing like a saloon in a mining boom town to bring in the money.

His only command was that the saloons be kept clean, that each had a piano, and that each had poker tables. He let the managers of the company he set up do the rest.

Three years later, as he finished the last details on his home in Tombstone Canyon, he was far, far richer than he had ever imagined being as a cattleman.

And that winter he stayed in his home in Tombstone Canyon. And only a few times did he go down to Roosevelt to play some poker.

~

New to the Thunder Mountain Series?
The first novel is available in electronic format
or print at your favorite booksellers.

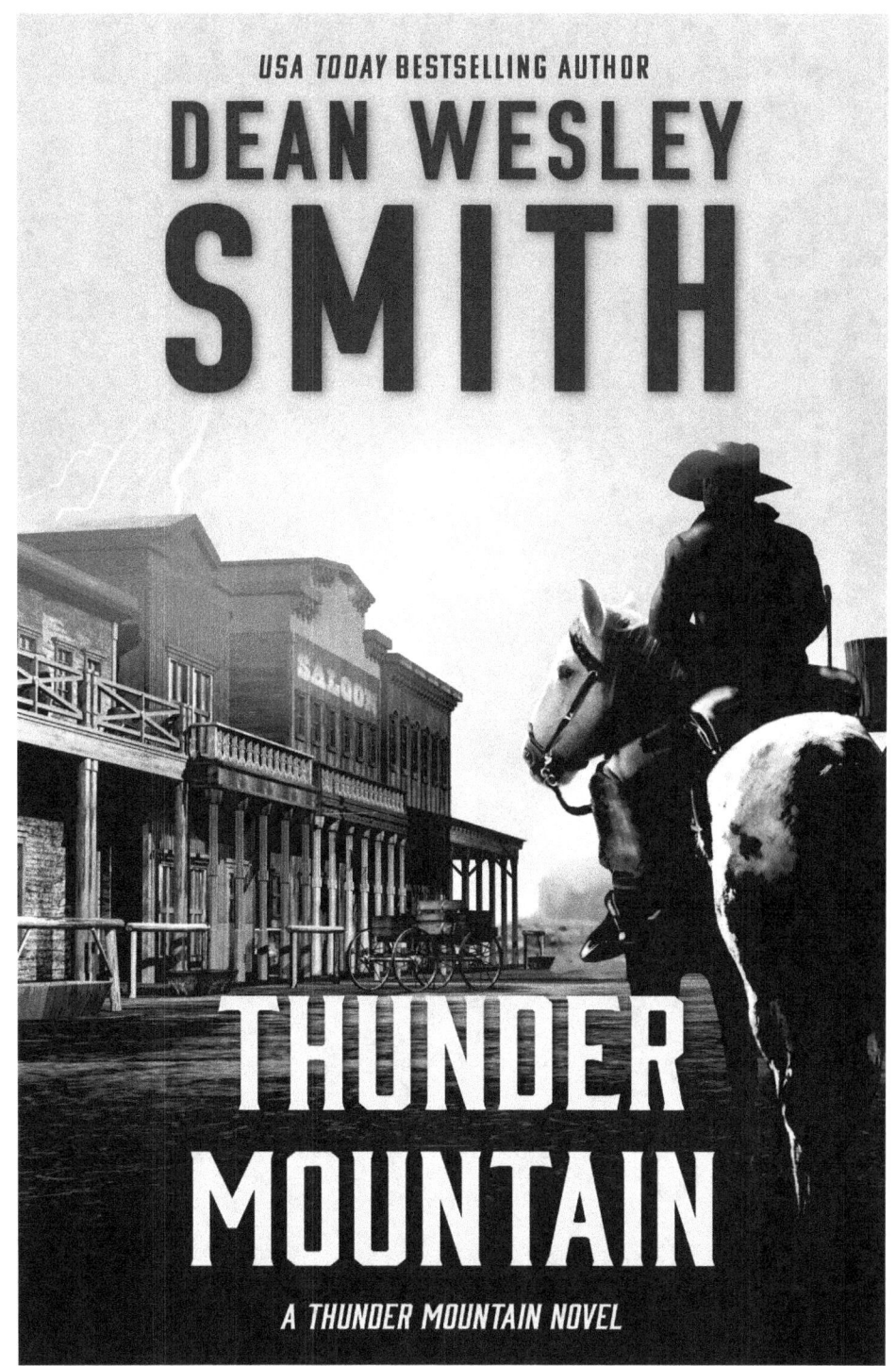

USA *Today* Bestselling Writer

DEAN WESLEY SMITH

THE LAST MAN

A Buckey The Space Pirate Story

Buckey the Space Pirate, over the years grew and met Fred, the talking Oak tree, and even got married.

But in his early years of youth, when he still wore his Space Pirate costume, Buckey explored some pretty strange new worlds.

In the classic Fredric Brown short story "Knock," aliens knock on the last man on Earth's door.

Buckey now knows what that man felt like. Only Fredric Brown never imagined the aliens to be like the woman Buckey found on the other side of the door.

A little warning. In Buckey's early days, sex happened.

THE LAST MAN
A Very Early Buckey the Space Pirate Story

The last man on Earth sat alone in a room. There was a knock on the door...
—Fredric Brown "Knock"

ONE

THERE WAS A knock at the hotel room door.

A faint, feminine knock.

"Don't panic now, Buckey, you old space pirate," I said to myself out loud. "It might be the wrong room."

I said that.

 Out loud.

I really did.

Another faint knock.

I couldn't believe I was doing this. Me, Buckey, the last man on Earth.

Alone in a room.

With someone knocking at the door.

Exactly like the old Fredric Brown science fiction story.

Damn Molly, anyway.

This was all her doing.

A simple costume party. That's how it all started. Just a simple party at a co-worker's house in one of those subdivisions that smelled of mowed lawns and sounded like young children on tricycles.

In this particular subdivision, the owners had had enough money to build houses that didn't look exactly alike, but not enough to really hide the similarity with massive amounts of walls, shrubs and trees.

Middle income, I think it's called.

Chances were it was going to be a boring party, so I had decided that I would try to liven things up with Buckey.

Not that Buckey hadn't been out of the closet before. He had, but only at last year's SuperBigCon science fiction convention. I figured people who didn't know anything about science fiction would think him wild.

In reality, Buckey's white boots, white tights, giant-plumed white hat, and jewel-studded saber were pretty tame at sf conventions. There the costumes tended to run from merchants from Zantar's three red suns to the belly dancers of Cain, who wore only small flashing lights in strategic places.

Those lights could really hypnotize a guy, let me tell you.

I ended up right about the suburban costumes. There were a lot of men dressed as gorillas, women dressed in Victorian dresses with small black masks,

and one couple dressed as Groucho and Harpo Marx.

Buckey really stood out.

Except for Molly.

TWO

ANOTHER KNOCK AT the door.

This time harder, more insistent.

I licked my lips and tried not to think about the dry taste in my mouth. Every time I got nervous, my mouth dried up like a desert. Only this time, I didn't know whether to be excited or afraid. I was Molly's last man on Earth, alone in a room. Should I let whoever was knocking in?

Or just sit here?

What did Fredric Brown do in his story? I think he just had his character say "Come in."

I didn't want to do that yet.

I just hoped it was Molly knocking.

It was supposed to be. It was her room.

It was her idea.

I first saw Molly while talking to a woman dressed like Queen Anne. The Queen had great breasts and the dress pushed them together and up and made the soft skin seem like it was about to explode.

The dress seemed to be straining to hold them back and I was making a play at being on stage when the dress let go.

Then Molly walked in.

Actually, she did more than walk in. She made an entrance.

She couldn't have done better with trumpets blaring. Every male head, including all the gorillas', turned to watch her.

She wore what I suppose could be called an alien costume. But not just any *Star Wars* or *Star Trek* alien costume. No way. It was a costume like none I'd ever seen.

And after years of going to science fiction conventions, I'd seen a lot of them.

Two well-muscled men, dressed as slaves and wearing only loin cloths, backed into the room in front of her, sprinkling small flower petals on the shag carpet and showing lots of cheek.

Molly wore a crown of pearls embedded in gold. Golden stands of hair flowed from under the crown and formed a triangle directly in the middle of her forehead pointing down her nose. She had large blue eyes, no eyebrows, and pearls hanging from her ears.

I figured right then that whatever she used to cover the rest of her body had to have been painted on. A complete flesh-toned suit.

But no matter how hard I stared, and trust me, I stared, I couldn't see any sign of nipples, belly button, or pubic hair.

Damn thick paint.

Most amazing costume I had ever seen.

Buckey Junior liked it a lot. He perked right to life.

"I am Maiden Molly," she said, and her voice, soft and husky, made Buckey Junior twitch even more. "I'm the Sex Queen of the planet Frost. I'm here looking for the last man on Earth."

"Right here, my lady," I heard myself shout before I even had time to think.

I strode across the room with the biggest strides I could take, left hand resting on my saber.

I reached her, pulled my plumed white hat off with a flourish, and did a deep waist bow in front of her. "Buckey the Space Pirate, at your service, your Majesty."

I had more courage than I thought I had. Who knew?

She looked me up and down, taking in my saber, my boots and where Buckey Junior saluted her costume.

Then she nodded slowly.

"Yes," she said. "Yes indeed. You might very well be the one."

Lucky me. But now what the hell was I going to do?

"Thank you, my lady," I said as best I could with my suddenly dry mouth.

For good measure, I did another deep waist bow, brushing my plumes across the floor.

I let my eyes move slowly up her costume as I stood. Not one sign of a seam in the cloth or for that matter, even the cloth itself. It was skin tight from her toes to her hair and hid everything without exception.

And I knew exactly what I was looking for.

"You will be tested," she said. "To see if you really are the last man on Earth. Meet me. One hour."

"But, where?"

———

She nodded her head slightly at one of her muscle men and he handed me a hotel room key. The key was for room twenty-three in the Flamingo Hotel. That was about five miles from here. A nice place. Not the best in town, but not cheap.

"Do not be late," she said and turned and left as the other men and gorillas cheered.

I stood open-mouthed, watching, as her royal ass swayed out the front door, followed closely by her two henchmen.

I looked back down at the key. I just hoped the two servants weren't invited to the test.

I made it to room twenty-three in less than half an hour.

THREE

ANOTHER KNOCK.

Now, I didn't really know if I wanted to go through with it. Old Buckey Junior still liked the idea of peeling off that skin tight costume and getting to those hidden secrets, but part of my mind kept trying to tell me something wasn't right.

Another insistent knock.

Buckey Junior won.

I licked my lips. "Come in," I said, just like in the story.

A henchman opened the door and stepped back.

Maiden Molly walked slowly into the room, this time without flowers at her feet. She was still just as impressive.

The henchman pulled the door closed and stayed out in the hall.

Right then I noticed that she was damn tall. I stood six feet. She had to top six-six. She wore a peach smelling perfume and her breasts were even bigger

than I remembered from the party. Still no sign of nipples, though.

She looked me right in the eye and I looked right back. Her eyes were green, with slightly cat-like irises. Neat effect. I figured she did it with contacts.

After a long few seconds, I decided I had better just keep playing along with her game. After all, she had paid for the room.

I took off my hat and did another deep waist bow. "Your Majesty," I said. "It is an honor."

Buckey Junior was hoping it was going to be a lot more.

"Yes, I imagine it is," she said, not even cracking a smile. "Are you ready for your test?"

"And just what might that be?" I asked. Her attitude was turning Buckey Junior right off.

"To see if you are the last man on Earth. Now, get undressed and we will begin."

She reached up and took off her crown of gold and pearls and set it carefully on the nightstand beside the bed. Her hair was soft, peach-fuzz looking, and it became obvious that the triangle of hair on her forehead was going to stay right in place.

Weird woman.

I laid my hat on the chair beside the television.

She turned and faced me. Slowly, her body started to glow a faint orange. Her skin seemed to be melting right before my eyes.

I blinked as hard as I could, but it didn't stop what I was seeing.

Slowly, large pink nipples formed on her breasts, her bellybutton sunk into place, and blonde soft hair appeared between her legs.

"Wow!" I said. "How'd you do that?"

"You are not undressed," she said. "How can we start?"

She moved to the head of the bed and stripped the bedspread and sheets from the bed.

I stared at her beautiful ass, huge chest, and soft skin. No matter how that costume worked, there was no way I was going to pass this up. Besides, Buckey Junior was screaming to be let out.

It took a long ten seconds to get out of the rest of my costume.

"Join me," she said and patted the bed.

I tried to remain as dignified as I could as I sat down, but what I really wanted to do was take a running jump at her. Buckey Junior just remained standing at attention.

She reached over and took hold of Buckey Junior. Her hands felt warm. I let out a deep sigh and started to reach for her.

She stopped me. "The test will be to see if you have any control. Or, in other words, to see how long you can last. Understand?"

I nodded.

So did Buckey Junior.

"Then let's begin. Lay out flat."

I did as I was told without her ever letting go of Buckey Junior.

She knelt beside me and put her soft lips around Buckey Junior, sucking him quietly into her soft throat.

Right at that moment, I thought Buckey Junior was going to let me down. Not that I'd blame him. Not at all. It felt so damn good. But my mind screamed hold on.

Hold On!

And Buckey Junior held on.

Not that it wasn't touch and go there for a moment with her mouth moving slowly up and down and up and down. But Buckey Junior resisted doing his fire hose impression and let my mind take back over at least for the moment.

I reached out and pulled her hips toward my face. She hesitated for only a moment, then swung her leg up and over and sat down right on my nose.

Bullseye!

At that moment Buckey Junior almost went off unannounced. But somehow, he held on again and I started to explore the new world that covered my face. Maiden Molly stirred slightly as I made first contact and then began a slow, grinding motion with her hips.

I figured if I had died right at that moment, I wouldn't have to go anywhere to find heaven.

She kept up her vacuum pump imitation on Buckey Junior. I really don't know how Buckey Junior held on.

Absolutely amazing.

Finally, after what seemed like the shortest eternity that ever existed, Molly suddenly sat up, turned around and sat right down on Buckey Junior.

Again, another bullseye.

Buckey Junior shouted "Thank you!" right up my spine and through every nerve in my body.

Molly took my hands and placed them over her nipples, then started a slow belly dance number on Buckey Junior.

I let my hands do what came naturally and slowly Molly picked up speed.

After a short few minutes, Molly leaned forward, put her breasts against my face and started a fast up and down motion on Buckey Junior.

That was the end of the road for Buckey Junior.

Molly pumped faster and faster.

And finally Buckey Junior let go.

I saw stars swirling before my eyes and for a moment I really thought I was going to die.

But I didn't.

After a few more quick up and downs to make sure Buckey Junior was drained, Molly stopped, sat up and then stood beside the bed, leaving me and Buckey Junior feeling disappointed.

"You did not pass the test," she said.

"Huh?" I asked.

At that moment I was lucky to get that word out of my mouth.

I raised my head off the sheet and looked at her, which took all the energy I had left. I could still see stars spinning around the insides of my eyelids.

"You are not the last man on Earth," she said. "I am sorry."

Her skin glowed again and started to melt. Her nipples disappeared. She picked up her crown and carefully fitted it back on her head.

"How'd you do that? And what exactly did I do wrong?"

Not that I really cared. I'd had a great time. But her attitude was annoying.

And her costume had me worried.

"You did not last long enough. Just last week a baker in Nevada lasted forty minutes longer than you did. Unless I find someone better, he will be the last man on Earth. Not you. I am sorry."

"You mean the last man is the one who lasts the longest?"

"That is correct."

"Can I have another chance?" I patted the bed beside me. Buckey Junior gave a little jerk to show he was interested too.

"No. Only once per man."

She turned and headed for the door.

I watched her for a moment. I had to admit, this woman was kinky. Stranger than anyone I had met at a science fiction convention.

I sat quickly up in bed. "Wait!"

She stopped and turned.

"Just for my information," I said, "Could you tell me how close I came and why you are looking for this last man?"

"To be my mate, the King of the planet Frost. We have very long winters there. As for you…" She smiled for the very first time. "You did very well. Only seventeen men have lasted longer than you. Now, goodbye."

"Bye," I said weakly as she closed the door behind her with a sharp click.

Buckey, the Space Pirate, the seventeenth-from-the-last man on Earth sat alone in a room.

And after all that, I couldn't have done anything even if someone had knocked.

Now Available
from all your favorite booksellers
in trade paper and electronic editions.

USA TODAY BESTSELLING AUTHOR

DEAN WESLEY SMITH

DRY CREEK CROSSING

A THUNDER MOUNTAIN NOVEL

Concord Coaches hold a mythical place in the history of the Old West. Colfax Shaw and Anna Taber, born a hundred years apart, find a compatible interest in one old Concord.

Anna studies the math of situations and timelines while Colfax focuses on the history of it all.

But both the math and the history, normally solid and dependable for both Anna and Colfax, suddenly become erratic. All because of a Concord stagecoach.

Another exciting novel in the Thunder Mountain series.

DRY CREEK CROSSING
A Thunder Mountain Novel

For Kris
Thanks for keeping me on track with these books

PART ONE
A Strange Connection

PROLOGUE

August 31st, 2017
The foothills west of Boise, Idaho

"HANG ON!" JACK shouted to his boss, Steph, who was working the grader on the old hiking trail. They were expanding the trail so that it could be paved up to a campsite on the lower levels of Dry Creek.

Jack held up his hand and Steph ground the noisy, rumbling beast to a halt, a large pile of dirt and rock and sage in front of his blade where he had dug into a hillside.

The day around them was hot, even for the sagebrush-covered foothills above the Treasure Valley. The temperature had to have gone past a hundred by ten in the morning. Who knew what it was now at two in the afternoon. Too hot, as far as Jack was concerned.

Jack had on a wide-brimmed hat to shelter his face and a bandana he kept tied around his neck and soaked with cold water. He had on a white, sweat-stained T-shirt, and jeans and work boots.

He stood five-six and was married to his childhood sweetheart, Patricia. They had two great kids. Patricia taught kindergarten in the Meridian area and they had a nice home not far from here in Eagle that he was very proud of and kept up, spending time each weekend on one project or another. He loved that home.

Most of the time, when working, he had a shovel in his hand and today was no exception. Under his jeans he wore leather wraps from the tops of his heavy work boots up to his knees to avoid snakebites.

Rattlers in this brush and rock this time of the year were everywhere and he had had more than one strike at his leg when he wasn't paying enough attention or the grader noise covered up their warning rattles.

A couple times the grader had uncovered entire nests of them. That could give a guy a start, that was for sure.

When he saw one, he just chopped off its head with the shovel. He always threatened to bring a couple home for dinner, but Patricia promised divorce if he did that.

On a day like today, he went through a bottle of water every fifteen to thirty minutes just to stay hydrated. Worth working in this heat since this job paid so well. He had been doing it now for six years and he had no real complaints. Working out in the elements in the dead of winter was much worse than the heat and the snakes.

He stepped forward to look at what he had seen Steph dig up with the grader. It was a worn piece of smooth wood, long and curved. It looked like it might have been polished at one time.

And beside it was what was clearly part of a very large wagon wheel of some sort. Jack dug with his shovel around in the dirt a little more and found more pieces and some thick old leather strips.

He motioned for Steph to back up the grader and park it and shut it down. They were clearly done for the day until someone got out here and looked at what they had found. Historians would dig it out and give them the all clear when they could go back to work.

And then for a week after they started working again, someone from the historical society would be watching to see if they found more.

Historical relics in Idaho had become very important in the last ten years and were things he and Steph bumped into about once every two months. It always got them some paid time off before they could go back to work. And they often got complimented when they didn't do much damage to the site they had found.

Jack figured he got Steph stopped soon enough this time to make the historians happy.

These hills and the area around Boise were full of all kinds of history, from Native American settlements to early mining to the Oregon Trail camps. From what Steph had told Jack, the Oregon Trail was just about two miles from where they were right now, down closer to the Boise River.

Amazing stuff and actually Jack found most of it interesting. Steph was teaching him more and more about it all the time.

Jack dug a little more and realized this was either a large wagon or a stagecoach. Steph had told him the other day that they were on or near the old Kelton Road, a major route for stages and wagons back in the late 1800s and early 1900s. But no telling why a wagon or stage would have been left here, up on the hill in the brush and scrub like this.

Steph had shut off the grader, leaving the sounds of the hot wind blowing through the sagebrush as the only noise.

He had on the same type of hat and wet bandana around his neck that Jack wore. And as Steph walked toward Jack, he poured more water over his bandana and then took a large drink.

Working the ground part of the two-man crew was hot, but being up on that grader was much worse. Jack was more than happy to be the shovel man.

Steph took one look at the remains and shook his head, using Jack's shovel to move a few things around.

Steph was far, far smarter about the historical stuff than Jack was. Steph had even graduated from the University of Idaho with a history degree.

Jack had barely made it out of Emmett High.

"If I didn't know better," Steph said, "I would swear this was a Concord stagecoach. See the thick leather straps?"

Jack nodded.

"Those were used like shock absorbers on the Concords. This is quite a find."

"But what is it doing up here?" Jack asked.

Steph looked around, then shook his head with a puzzled frown. "Not a clue, actually. See that cut in the side of the hill about a hundred yards down?"

Jack could see what he was talking about. That was a cut done when they built a trail or a road.

"That's the remains of the old main road over to Freezeout back in the days of this coach," Steph said. "No idea why a Concord Coach would be this far off the trail."

"Looks like the historians have a real puzzle on their hands," Jack said.

Steph pulled out his phone and hit a number, then as he was waiting for the person on the other end to answer, he said, "They sure do. A whopper."

ONE

September 4th, 2017
Boise, Idaho

COLFAX SHAW WALKED into the large cavern under the Historical Institute in Boise, Idaho. He expected it to be empty, but the founders of the Institute, mathematicians Duster and Bonnie Kendal were sitting at the large kitchen counter eating. And the place had a thick, rich scent of peanut butter cookies someone must have baked just recently.

The cavern had high stone ceilings and the flat stone floor was covered with scattered cloth couches and chair groupings for private conversations. They were all in brown tones, as were the area rugs under them. Each area had a couple lamps, and one large group of couches and chairs faced a massive stone wood-burning fireplace.

It was still hot outside and the fireplace wasn't lit. In a month or so it would be and the cavern all winter would have that wonderful smell of burning wood.

Right now, to Colfax, it felt cool and inviting, since he had just come in from the late summer's heat.

A massive kitchen had been built along the far wall of the cavern and a counter that could sit thirty people ran along the wall in front of ovens and stoves and fridges. Just under thirty people knew about this cavern at his point in time, but when Colfax asked why the place was so big his first time down here, Duster said, "You ought to see how busy this place is in three hundred years. So we built it for then, not now."

Colfax hadn't understood that completely at the time. He wasn't sure he understood it yet. They had built this place in the early 1880s with the 2280s in mind. That was some amazing planning.

The three Victorian mansions over the top of this cavern were the first three homes built way out on Warm Springs Avenue, back when it was nothing more than a rutted wagon trail along the Boise River. Now the three homes were stately manors, the official home of the Historical Research Institute.

Colfax had only known about this secret cavern for about a year now, since Bonnie and Duster and Dawn Edwards and Madison Rogers, the four that ran the Institute, invited him into the secret part.

He actually was the director of the Idaho Historical Society and he had used the Institute's library and research facilities for two years before he was invited down here.

Even though it was only a year ago in this timeline, it felt like ages. He had lived over eight hundred years in the past in that year of real time. Each trip into the past of another timeline, no matter how long he was gone or what happened to him, only lasted two minutes and fifteen seconds here.

He loved that wonderful part about traveling into the past.

And he loved seeing history first hand. It made his work both at the historical society and the research for his books much, much richer.

He had no idea how old Bonnie and Duster actually were. More than likely more thousands of years older than he wanted to think about. Duster had become a marshal in many Old West towns and his picture showed up regularly in historical records.

"Hi, folks," Colfax said when he was about halfway across the cavern. He didn't want to surprise Bonnie and Duster.

Both of them glanced around and smiled.

"Join us for lunch?" Bonnie asked.

"Headed back," Colfax said, "so just ate before I left my office. Thanks."

Colfax stood six-one and Duster was basically the same height. But while Colfax looked like he could add a few pounds on his thin frame, Duster was all muscle and wide shoulders. Duster always wore a long brown oilcloth duster and a cowboy hat and boots, although at the moment the hat and coat were draped over another stool at the kitchen counter.

Bonnie had long brown hair that she usually kept pulled back. She always seemed to wear a nice silk blouse, jeans, and running shoes, and today was no exception.

Colfax never dressed up even to that level. He liked the old work shirts with the sleeves rolled up, jeans, and tennis shoes or cowboy boots.

Neither Bonnie or Duster looked much older than thirty-five and yet Colfax knew they were two of the smartest minds on the planet. Maybe the smartest, at least in mathematics and physics.

And they both loved history and had funded up this Institute, as well as many chairs in universities and construction projects all over the country. When they brought in a historian to the Institute to work on a project, they paid all the historian's expenses, gave them free food, and a huge salary, and wanted no credit or copyright on the property researched.

Most historians coming in just stayed for a few years and then left never knowing about the cavern and the ability to travel back into the history of other timelines.

It seems that Bonnie and Duster only invited into the cavern those with an intense passion for history. A burning passion, as Duster had said. Colfax knew he fit that bill in more ways than one.

And traveling in the past in other timelines was a perfect way to research history. No one could go back in time in this timeline, but the other timelines were basically, for all intents and purposes, identical to this one. So the history of one timeline they traveled was the history of another.

And if the traveler changed something in the past, it just started a new timeline. From what Colfax understood of what Bonnie and Duster had explained to him, the timelines were infinite, with an infinite number being created every moment in time. The math of that, at a certain point, went past his historical mind.

"Where you headed to?" Duster asked.

"Actually," Colfax said as he moved around the counter to a fridge and got a bottle of water, "just here in Boise in 1902. Did you hear about the remains of a Concord Coach they found up near Dry Creek last week?"

Both Bonnie and Duster looked up with the exact same expression on their faces.

"A crew expanding the trail up to the lower Dry Creek campground uncovered it about a hundred yards above the old Kelton Road."

"What in the world was it doing up there?" Duster asked.

Colfax just smiled and raised his hands. "Why I'm heading back, to find out the answer to that very question."

"And no historical record of a stage going missing?" Bonnie asked.

"Nothing in the papers or local reports from around the area," Colfax said.

Since his people from the historical society went up to help with the digging up of the stage, he had spent the last three days looking for any reference. Nothing, and there should have been one. Concord stagecoaches were used on that route to help get train passengers from Boise up into the Payette Valley.

They were big, heavy, and expensive coaches, but considered the top of the line for stagecoaches.

From what he could find, the stages had run once a week, taking three days to get up to the New Meadows area, three days to get back in the spring, summer, and early fall months, when the weather allowed.

The schedule had stopped in the fall of 1902 and the transit company shut down without any known reason. Colfax was betting that was when the stage ended up on that hillside. His first and best clue, so that was where he was going.

Bonnie turned to Duster. "A Concord gone missing or not gone missing. Does that remind you of something?"

Duster thought for a moment, then laughed. "Dr. Taber's project, of course."

Colfax suddenly felt very confused, which actually wasn't that unusual around Bonnie and Duster. Their minds just worked out in places the rest of the race didn't go.

"Dr. Taber's project?" Colfax asked.

"Dr. Anna Taber," Bonnie said. "She's an amazing mathematician from a hundred years in the future. That's her base timeline."

"Since we have a ton better computers by that point," Duster said, "Anna's idea was to study data from one simple event in 1902 and then gather data from a vast number of timelines and hundreds of travelers to see how the math worked from that one event on future events."

Bonnie smiled at what must have been Colfax's puzzled frown. "She's doing basic timeline study."

"The Concord on that hill is her event?" Colfax asked, stunned.

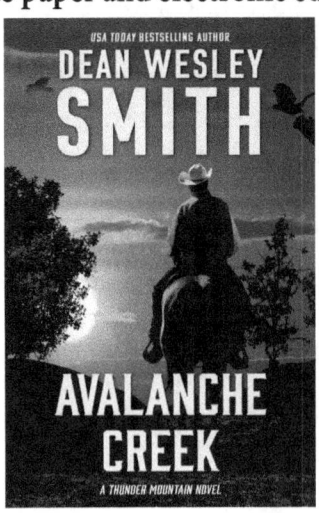
He still didn't have all this time travel thinking down completely yet, so the idea of a woman from a hundred years in the future studying something they'd just found in 2017 was amazing. Of course, he had been planning on going back to find out more about what happened as well, so a hundred years in the future wouldn't be much different.

"It is her event," Bonnie said, nodding and continuing to eat. "She just got approval from Director Parks to go all the way back to 1902, if I remember the meeting right. He was going to go with her for a day to help her get settled."

Duster nodded and kept eating.

Colfax remembered one of the rules the Institute had about a traveler needing special permission to go back more than one hundred years from before this time. If Dr. Taber was from a hundred years in the future, her limit should be today.

"So she got the permission to go to 1902?" Colfax asked.

"She did," Duster said. "Just in the last day or so."

"In fact," Bonnie said, " because of her research, she moves around through the four hundred years of the Institute more than anyone but Director Parks."

"Wow," Colfax said.

"Might want to try to find her in 1902," Duster said. "Give her a few pointers on living in that time. She seemed real nervous about going back there."

Bonnie nodded. "She does seem to be out of her element back there, from what Director Parks has told me."

"Any idea where she might be?" Colfax asked, not really sure if he wanted to find her or not.

"Hold on," Bonnie said and took out her cell phone and hit a number. After a moment she said, "Dr. Shaw is headed back to 1902 to investigate the same event that Dr. Taber picked. Did she tell you exactly the time and place she was headed?"

After a moment Bonnie laughed and said thanks and hung up.

"Director Parks went back with her to show her a few ropes of the time. Seems this is the first time she has been back that far. He said it would be great if you could help her out."

Colfax nodded. "Glad to."

"She went back to August 3rd 1902 and Parks stayed with her until the 5th, but he's betting she will remain holed up here in the cavern for a while, so if you jump back to the 6th, you should find her."

"Get her to move down to the Idanha," Duster said. "Best way to get used to the time period."

"I'll do that," Colfax said. He had been meaning to jump back to September and stay at the Idanha, so going a month early wouldn't matter at all. And she might know more about the event than he did, considering the time she was from.

"Have a fun trip," Bonnie said, turning back to her lunch.

Colfax nodded and turned and headed for the door that would take him down to the prep room for 1902 and then to the crystals that were other timelines that would allow him to jump back in time.

"Good luck when you meet her," Duster said, laughing.

Bonnie whacked his arm and Duster laughed even more.

Colfax stopped and looked back. "Am I going to be the one who needs the help?"

Duster laughed again and waved his hand. "We'll still be here eating lunch when you get back. Let us know how it goes."

"She's wonderful," Bonnie said. "Don't worry."

Colfax just shook his head. He wasn't sure if he wanted to meet this future Anna. But looked like he was going to one way or another. But first, he wanted to find out why that Concord Coach was on that hill.

He knew the puzzle might have him staying for years in the past, but for Bonnie and Duster, he would be back before they finished lunch.

And sometimes, even after doing this for hundreds of years in the past, that time difference still struck him as hard to comprehend.

And he was going back over a hundred years to meet a mathematician from over a hundred years in the future.

Yeah, this never got confusing.

But it seemed this Dr. Taber understood it completely and was studying the math of it. No wonder she had trouble with the past. He had a hunch that advanced math and 1902 just often didn't go together.

TWO

August 6th, 1902
Boise, Idaho

ANNA TABER HAD managed, this time, to not fall off the horse in the short two circles around the Institute grounds. Yesterday she had fallen off twice. Luckily no one had been watching.

She only stood five-two and getting on those beasts was a chore, let alone staying on one. Not once in all her years in the university systems did anyone ever tell her she would need to learn how to ride a horse to be a mathematician.

Not one damn time.

Luckily, one of the stable hands who worked for the Institute had helped her with her horse and with how to take care of it. The man was of this time and had no idea she wasn't, so she had to be careful and Director Parks had set up the help before he left, thankfully.

She was staying in one of the large suites upstairs in the old Victorian with a feather bed that was impossible to climb out of because it was so damned comfortable. But since they kept the Victorian to the time period, and occasionally there was a local-time person cleaning or doing work on the Victorian mansion, she was showering and mostly living in the cavern and wearing her normal clothes while in the cavern.

She had set up camp on a group of the large sofas near the massive stone fireplace and Director Parks had shown her how to light the thing. She felt a great accomplishment being able to do at least that much.

Two nights in a row she had had a fire and it had been wonderful. She had sat sipping hot tea, reading, and eating fresh peanut butter cookies she had baked herself.

She had always eaten peanut butter cookies, especially in times of stress. In college only running a ton of miles every day kept the pounds off from all the cookies.

Director Parks was the one who had suggested she stay here at the Institute for a time, practice some on riding, and also do a little more research on how women were supposed to act and dress in this time period. So she had books from the library upstairs spread out around her couches.

She loved this big cavern. It had a bunch of traffic in her home timeline of 2117, and in 2217 it was often noisy from conversations of all the scientists from different periods of time talking.

Here, in 1902, no one had even come into the big cavern in the day since Director Parks left. Except for a few stable workers outside who she had to be careful talking with, she hadn't seen anyone at all.

So she had time to read and research, something she loved to do.

In her research, she had discovered that this time period for women, especially in the west, was a nightmare as far as she was concerned. Repressed and rule-bound didn't begin to describe it. Yet women were the core of the time, the center of every household, and women owned and ran businesses of all types.

A very strange mix.

And she had come to realize that she would need a cover story. She was going to need to come up with that before she ventured into Boise and then on west of the growing town to try to find out more about that old Concord stagecoach.

She had notes on creating that cover, but so far had found no story that really fit her for a woman her age, with money, traveling alone. She just looked too young to be alone, even though her real age was thirty-four and she had lived more centuries in other timelines than she wanted to think about.

If she didn't get a cover story figured out, she would jump back to 2017 and talk with the director and maybe Bonnie and Duster about that. Bonnie would be able to give her some ideas.

Anna had just finished showering after her successful, but short ride, and had her bright red hair dried and back up on her head like she liked to wear it. She was dressed in her normal jeans, short-sleeved running shirt, and tennis shoes.

She was just taking the daily batch of peanut butter cookies out of the old stove when she heard a voice.

"Anyone home?"

She stepped away from the stove against the inside wall of the cavern and saw a man coming from the prep room and crystals. Only he was still dressed like he must dress in the future, in a work shirt with the sleeves rolled up, jeans, and tennis shoes.

And wow was he good looking.

Wow, just wow.

He was tall, very thin, and had an infectious grin on his face that showed a full set of teeth. He had a thin nose that seemed to barely hold up his wire rim glasses.

"Dr. Taber I presume?" he said, walking toward her. "Bonnie and Duster told me I might find you here. And holy cow does this place smell great!"

"Fresh batch of peanut butter cookies," she said, pointing to the hot pan sitting on the stove. "Would you like one?"

"I would love one," he said. "My favorite. My grandmother used to make them every time we visited. But didn't know peanut butter was a going thing by this point in history."

She scooped up a cookie and put it on a napkin and handed it to him, then took one for herself.

"It was," she said, smiling. "Not machine made yet, but it has existed for a decade or so, but I brought this peanut butter from the future. Director Parks made me swear to not tell anyone, and I have now broken that promise."

He smiled and stuck out his hand. "Not a word from me. I'm Colfax Shaw, director of the Idaho Historical Society in 2017. Just call me Colfax."

She took his hand and was shocked at her reaction to his strength and wonderful smile.

"Anna Taber, mathematician from 2117. Great to meet you. Call me Anna, if you would."

"I would love to," he said, looking into her eyes.

Oh, god, his brown eyes could melt a person.

More Thunder Mountain Novels
Available at your favorite booksellers.

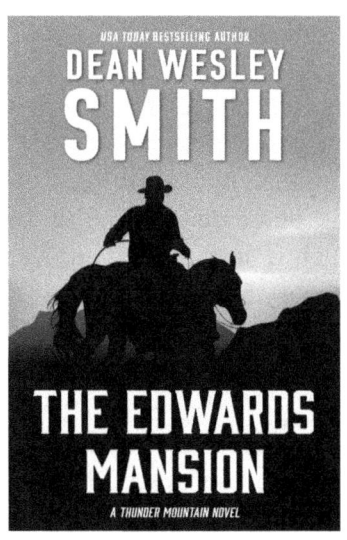

She didn't want to let go of his hand and stop looking up into those wonderful deep-brown eyes behind his glasses, but she finally did a half second before it got really awkward.

Or maybe a half second after.

Didn't matter, still too soon.

He looked away and took a bite of the cookie, then glanced around the cavern. "I sure miss the kitchen counter in this time period."

She nodded. There were only a few wooden kitchen tables near the stoves and cutting areas. She indicated he should come with her.

"I made a nest over here on the couches. Been doing some research into this time period."

"They said it was your first time back. You like it?" he asked as he dropped down on a couch across from where she sat and put his feet up on the wooden coffee table. He looked very relaxed as he took another bite of the cookie.

"First time," she said, nodding. "And I must say that I made it two laps around the grounds without falling off a horse today."

She thought he was going to choke on the cookie crumbs from laughing. His laugh was wonderful. Deep and rich and full of warmth. She had met a lot of travelers over the hundreds of years she had traveled through timelines, but had never had an attraction to one before now.

"Sorry," he said after he coughed a few times. "Didn't mean to laugh at your accomplishment."

He sort of stressed the world "accomplishment" which made her laugh as well.

"Riding horses is not something they teach in higher math classes in 2117."

"Yeah, I can understand that," he said. "Honestly it took me a couple of weeks of practice on horses my first time back here to get comfortable as well."

"Thank you for easing my shame," she said, smiling at him and he smiled back.

"So Bonnie and Duster tell me we are coming at the same incident from a hundred years apart," he said.

"The Concord stagecoach?" she asked.

That surprised her. That was such a minor event, she never expected any other traveler to be interested.

He nodded. "I came from September 2017. They just found the wreckage of the Concord a week ago in my time. I was coming back to try to figure out how it ended up on that hill. Not a word about it in any papers of this time."

"In my time they don't know why it ended up on the hill either," she said. "It seems to be a forgotten little detail that has two outcomes, from what I understand."

He sat up straight in the chair, his eyes taking on a new level of intensity that she liked a lot. This guy clearly had a lot of levels about him.

"Two outcomes?"

She nodded, finding it enjoyable to actually talk with someone besides Director Parks about her project.

"The first outcome is the mystery," she said, "about how the big coach ended up on that steep hill above the old road and got buried for a hundred years."

He nodded to that, but said nothing.

"The second outcome in some timelines is the coach didn't get buried, but instead made it to the New Meadows, Idaho area."

"Seriously?" he asked. "The same coach?"

She nodded. "It seems that way. Not one hundred percent sure yet. It was stored until a kid decided to rebuild it. In those timelines it sits in your Historical Society on display."

She watched the shocked look on Colfax's handsome face. He just sat staring off into space, clearly thinking.

And she didn't mind at all because she just kept staring at him.

THREE

August 6th, 1902
Boise, Idaho

COLFAX HAD BEEN shocked when he entered the big cavern to be greeted by the rich, thick, wonderful smell of peanut butter cookies and the bright green eyes and striking red hair of Anna Taber.

He didn't know what he was expecting, but it sure wasn't a tiny, strikingly beautiful woman with a smile that could melt an iceberg from a hundred miles away.

She couldn't have been much more than five foot, maybe five-two, and had her bright red hair tied up on the top of her head in some fashion that added a few inches to her.

The jeans and running shirt gave her an athletic look and she didn't have an extra ounce of fat on her. That much was clear from the tight shirt and jeans.

And their first handshake was something he couldn't even imagine. He had had his share of girlfriends over the years, but none of them seemed to put up with his focus and drive very long.

And over the past hundreds of years living back here in the past, he had had a few relationships that had lasted, but after they were done, he had never wanted to return to them in another timeline to do them again.

But that handshake was something special. He flat didn't want to let go of her hand and she didn't seem to want to pull away either.

This kind of instant attraction to another traveler surprised him.

Scared him a little as well.

And under normal circumstances, he would have become a shy, sort of tall, bumbling fool. But with the fantastic cookie and the story that she hadn't fallen off a horse today, he had relaxed.

He felt comfortable with her, and that also surprised him.

"So why study this one event and the possible timelines?" he asked after she had explained a little more about the two outcomes of that Concord Coach.

She looked at him and suddenly he could sense a worry in her bright green eyes. And he had no idea at all what she would be worried about.

"Not sure how much Bonnie and Duster told you about me," she said after a moment, avoiding his question.

"Not much, actually," he said. "I just ran into them here in the cavern as I was headed out and told them about the Concord find and they remembered you were studying that as well. So Duster called Parks to get the date you would be here and I jumped back here to this time to talk with you."

She nodded, so he went on.

"Bonnie said you were from 2117, but that you jumped all over the four hundred plus years of the Institute timeline, working on the math of different timelines. At that point, I must admit, I got confused and intimidated."

She laughed and clearly relaxed.

"History major," he said, shrugging. "Math was something we had to take to get past the first year."

She laughed again and then said, "To be honest, I would have flunked the one and only history class I was forced to take if it wasn't for a friend and a lot of pizza."

"Now look at us," he said, indicating the cavern around them, "sitting like rats in a cave. How far we've come."

She laughed once again and he just let himself enjoy it. It was real, deep for her size and seemed to come from the heart as well as the mind.

He was just damned glad he could make her laugh.

"Okay," she said, "to answer your question, that Concord Coach, from what I can tell, is a major turning point in the history of humanity. Again, not completely sure, but it seems like a focus point in time."

He dropped his feet off the coffee table and sat up straight. "You lost me and I didn't even hear any math."

She smiled. "Every major person who brings progress to humanity has had a lot of turning points in their lives."

He nodded. He understood that.

She went on. "Einstein, Bell, Jobs, and so on. In 1973 a young kid by the name of Ryder Marks in the New Meadows region finds that Concord in a barn. From what we have been able to learn, he gets interested, restores it over years of work, and goes on to college where he meets a young woman, marries her and they have three kids."

He just nods, following her so far.

"One of their great, great grandkids in 2136 becomes one of those major turning point people. The great, great grandkid invents a form of anti-gravity that revolutionizes the ability to get into space, changes plane flight, energy use, you name it. Solves a ton of the world's problems."

Now Colfax understood. "So you think that if that Concord isn't in that barn, the Ryder kid doesn't get interested in saving it and doesn't end up in college?"

Anna nods. "That is the theory. And only some rough math pointing that way. Without college, Ryder Marks stays on his family's small ranch, marries a high school sweetheart, has three kids, and from what we can find the line does nothing going forward but live good, solid lives."

"And no one else invents this anti-gravity thing?"

Anna shook her head. "No, in fact, I have been as far forward as the Institute goes, which is to 2317, and without that invention, a lot of problems on this planet don't get solved."

"Wow," Colfax said, shaking his head. "All from an event we don't even know why it happened."

"Exactly," Anna said. "My project is to do the math on all of this, try to make sense out of the infinite timelines of possibilities that stem from that Concord Coach ending up on that hill or not."

Colfax nodded and they sat there for a moment.

Then he finally asked the question he hoped she wouldn't turn down.

"Would you like some help from a historian?"

She beamed. "I would love it."

"On one condition," he said.

She frowned, but nodded.

"You keep making those fantastic cookies."

She laughed and reached over to shake his hand.

"Deal."

He shook her hand and once again flat didn't want to let go.

But he did.

And they got two new cookies to celebrate their working partnership.

FOUR

August 10th, 1902
Boise, Idaho

ANNA WAS FINALLY starting to feel comfortable on the back of a horse. Colfax had helped her a lot. He was so tall, he could just walk beside her while she was on the horse and talk her into relaxing and not fighting the poor beast.

She had even started to like her horse and had named her Seshat after the ancient god of math.

Colfax told her he thought that was a great name for the horse, but he was pretty sure that Seshat was the god of astronomy and bookkeeping.

She had laughed and said, "Close enough."

She loved how over the last four days, Colfax had made her laugh. She didn't remember just enjoying time so much with anyone before.

Last night, after she had gotten finished with her work and he had cooked them both dinner, she had showed him her fire-building skills. They had sat in front of the fire and just talked until finally she staggered off to bed.

After the second day with Colfax, she had decided she really wanted him to join her in that massive feather bed. But so far he had been a perfect gentleman, damn him.

So now, today, they were going to go for a test into Boise. They were going to ride into town early in the morning, have breakfast in the Idanha Hotel, and get back to the Institute before it got too warm.

It was still pitch black outside when he tapped on her door to wake her.

"Come in," she remembered muttering.

She was not a good morning person, to say the least. And had never much had anyone around her when she woke up, which was always a good thing.

She sort of remembered he opened the door and then closed it, letting in some light from the hallway. Then he turned on one corner lamp in the suite.

"Rise and shine," he said. "If we're going to make breakfast."

She rolled over and kept the quilt up to her chin and her eyes closed. The feather bed just was so comfortable.

"Let's go for lunch."

He laughed, that sound she loved to hear. "Too hot. Remember, no air-conditioning."

She opened one eye and focused on him. He was smiling and dressed in his riding clothes, sitting in the chair across the room from the foot of her bed. He had helped her pick out her clothes for today, explaining they were the type of riding clothes a woman of means would wear. They were hanging in the bathroom.

He had suggested that this morning she only splash water on her face and wait to take a shower when they returned, since they would be covered in road dust and sweat when they got back.

"Are we really doing this," she said, glancing at the window. It was still pitch dark out there. Not even the birds in the trees were making any noise.

"We got to get you used to this time period," he said. "And a breakfast run is the best way to start doing that."

"You are such a meanie," she said. "Anyone ever tell you that?"

With that she tossed back the quilt like she normally did and went to get out of bed, realizing too late that she was totally naked.

He quickly stood and turned for the door, clearly embarrassed. "I'll wait outside while you get dressed."

She laughed as she stood up. "Don't you dare. You stay right there because I am going to need help getting into those things you call riding clothes."

She looked at him as he opened his mouth, then shut it. His eyes were wide.

Good, maybe later she could get him to scrub her back in the shower and they could release some of this building sexual tension. But first this stupid ride into town.

"You know it's dark out there," she said as she headed for the bathroom, completely naked. "Horses, I'm fairly certain, can't see in the dark."

He chuckled. "It will be light enough once we are ready to go."

"Good," she said, smiling at him. "I'll call when I need your help."

He was just standing there by the door, looking confused, a little shaken, and very damn handsome.

She closed the bathroom door and then smiled at herself in the mirror.

That wasn't planned, but she had a hunch it would turn out just wonderfully.

FIVE

August 10th, 1902
Boise, Idaho

THE MORNING AIR had a pretty good bite to it, and both Colfax and Anna had worn an extra coat and gloves that when in Boise they would leave in their saddle bags with the horses.

The sun was just cresting the eastern mountains when they reached the edge of town. All the way along, Anna kept trying to figure out where things would be in a hundred years or two hundred years. To her the buildings that would come up were like shadows in the early-morning light.

He finally got her to just stop doing that and enjoy the incredible unspoiled view of the winding wagon road along the river. The trees were lush and green and the complete lack of wind kept the morning silent except for a few birds and the sounds of their horses' hooves on the hard-packed dirt.

Anna was riding just fine, and they road side-by-side for most of the forty-minute ride and talked some. After about ten minutes she actually seemed relaxed.

However, he found himself distracted, unable to get that image of Anna standing naked, smiling at him, as if that was natural and happened every day.

He wanted it to happen every day.

She was beyond beautiful as far as he was concerned. A natural redhead, with a small chest, thin hips, and well-toned muscles.

He had hoped over the last few days that they might take their growing friendship to a relationship and seemed as if he hadn't been the only one of them thinking that way.

And that had been the only time so far he had seen her with her long, red hair down. It fell past her shoulders and looked like silk.

He was just proud of himself for not fainting when she climbed out of bed naked like that. That would have been embarrassing, but something six or seven hundred years of living ago, he might very well have done. Coming through college as a history major just didn't offer him much opportunity to meet women as attractive as Anna.

And back then women as attractive as Anna wouldn't have given him a second glance.

They got their horses into the Idanha Hotel stables, then walked the two blocks around the hotel to the front door, her arm tucked into his as if they were a couple.

"You know, in 2017," she said, looking up at the hotel, "this place is still impressive, but now, in this time, it is downright stunning."

He had to agree. The Idanha Hotel had been finished just a year before and the four stone and brick spires on the four corners were the tallest things in Boise. The exterior was mostly polished sandstone, the windows tall, and the building seemed to dominate an entire block of Main Street.

It was luxury for this time all the way. He always stayed here, usually in one of the big suites on the top floor. He flat loved it.

As they climbed the stone steps and went through the massive polished wood and glass front doors, Anna said simply, "Wow."

He always had the same feeling when coming into this lobby.

It was massive and around the room were furniture settings so people could sit and talk. Many of those settings were now occupied.

On one wall was a massive stone fireplace that vanished into the tall ceiling, while to the left across the lobby as they entered was a grand maple staircase that curved upward. Beside the staircase was a mass of steel and cages that was Idaho's first elevator. He could see the name Otis in big letters on the side.

Directly across from the entrance was a long, polished maple front desk with mailboxes on the wall behind it for guests.

The lobby had a good thirty people in it, all talking or reading newspapers. A few looked like, from their baggage, that they were checking out. The sound was of a low murmur and the place smelled of freshly-baked bread.

He steered Anna to the right and toward two open glass doors. The restaurant filled the right corner of the main floor of the Idanha and was about half full at the moment. The fresh-bread smell got stronger the closer they got, like a large hand pulling them in.

A man in a suit and tie greeted them as they entered with a slight bow.

"Two for your fine breakfast, please," Colfax said.

"With pleasure, sir," the man said, nodding, and leading them through the dining room to a seat near a massive stone fireplace that had no fire in it.

The tall windows that ran all the way to the ceiling were opened along the top and a cool breeze was flowing through the entire room.

They looked out over main street and the activity was picking up out there as people tried to get things done before the heat of the day set in.

Colfax held the chair for Anna and she smiled a thank you, then he ordered them both fresh orange juice and glasses of water with ice.

Ice in the summer was expensive, but by doing so he signaled to the restaurant staff that they had money.

Their clothes also gave that signal, since both of them were dressed as people of means.

"I thought I was going to faint by the time I got across this wonderful room," Anna said, leaning forward and whispering.

Colfax glanced around. There was no table of people close enough to them to overhear a conversation.

"You are doing great," he said. "Just relax and enjoy the food, especially the breads."

"Why?" Anna asked, looking puzzled.

"You ever met Megan and Carol? Two of the travelers for this time period."

Anna shook her head.

"Megan is the pastry chef here. Carol is a medical doctor from my time who managed to save her life. They fell in love and their wedding was amazing. Later tonight I'll tell you about it. Long, but amazing story of how time travel can be used to solve impossible problems."

"This is an impossibly wonderful situation," she said, indicating the beautiful

maple-paneled walls, tall windows, and light room.

"I love it here," he said. "We are sitting in history."

"No matter where we go in time," she said, "we are always sitting in history."

He had to nod agreement to that. She was exactly right.

"But," she said, looking around. "I have to admit this feels almost like a sacred place."

"Not so sure about sacred," Colfax laughed. "But most certainly beautiful. Like you were when you climbed out of bed this morning."

He couldn't believe he had been so bold to say that, but he just couldn't clear that wonderful sight from his mind. And really didn't want to, actually.

She actually blushed, the red flowing up into her bright hair, but she held his gaze. "You liked that, huh?"

"What was not to like?" he asked, smiling at her.

She blushed slightly again and smiled back.

He knew, right at that point, she had done that pretty much on purpose.

But before either of them could say anything more, they were saved by the waiter bringing them water and juice.

SIX

August 10th, 1902
Boise, Idaho

THE RIDE IN this morning had been stunningly beautiful. Anna had never realized how peaceful riding a horse could be. And thanks to Colfax, she had lost her fear of riding, which helped a lot.

Breakfast in the Idanha Hotel had been just amazing. Not only was the hotel and restaurant stunning architecture, but the food seemed to melt in her mouth and the rolls that came with breakfast were sinful.

And as far as she knew, she didn't make any social mistakes. She would have to ask Colfax later if he saw any.

She was actually starting to think that she might be able to survive a little in this time period, with a little more help.

But it felt great to have Colfax with her. She was so far out of her element it wasn't even funny.

Well, to Colfax, he made it funny in a wonderful way.

After breakfast it was clear the day was going to start heating up pretty soon, but they decided to see if they could find the stage office of the small company that ran the Concord on the line up to the New Meadows area and back. Colfax figured it would only take them about an hour out of the way.

After breakfast, Anna had donned a wide-brimmed hat to keep the sun off her too-white skin. And she had left her sleeves down long to her riding gloves.

She was going to be damned hot by the time they got back, but that was better than getting sunburned.

The headquarters for the small line was a barn tucked against the foothills with a small shack beside it. A hand-painted wooden sign hung over the doorway. "Adams Delivery and Stage."

They didn't stop, but Anna felt almost let down at the looks of it. So much in history seemed to turn on that Concord Coach and yet this was the place it left from. A place that looked like it was about to fall down.

She wasn't sure what she was expecting, actually. Maybe something more like the Idanha Hotel, with a mythic feel.

But it was just a shack.

"Was that kind of office normal for stage lines?" she asked Colfax as they wound through some trees heading back in the direction of the Institute.

"Pretty much," Colfax said. "Since the railways came in, the coach lines were only used for local routes and companies came and went quickly in the business. It will all pretty much be finished in another decade or so, an entire industry vanished into time."

Anna nodded. "Seems like time can be brutal on some things."

They rode in a comfortable silence for a time after that. Colfax seemed to have no problem with silence, one of the many, many things she was starting to really like about him.

At one point, Colfax pointed to a flat area near the Boise River. "The Institute already owns that land and that will be where they will build the major library in another forty-some years, after the Second World War."

"That library is an amazing place," Anna said, trying to imagine that massive, ten-story building sitting there. It also went down five floors underground and in her time had expanded out in both directions into other buildings, all connected by sky-bridges.

"Those of us who travel back to this time period are collecting books and newspapers for it all the time," he said. "We put it all in a massive cavern at the Institute to be brought out and sorted later when the library is built."

She looked over at him. "Seriously?"

"No way else to get a lot of the stuff for the library," he said. "I spent a couple hundred years back in this time period and before, finding old mining towns that had newspapers and buying up copies for the archives."

"Was that fun?" she asked, staring at him.

He smiled. "Actually, it was. And some of those local newspaper editors were amazing people. I keep meaning to write a book about some of them, but just can't seem to find the time."

At that, he laughed and she laughed with him. Time was certainly something they both had more than enough of.

"I think it would be a great book," she said. "Nothing like it."

"Thanks," he said, nodding.

Ten minutes later, at a little after eleven in the morning, they were handing off their horses to one of the stable hands behind the Institute.

Anna felt only slightly sore from the longish ride, but not as bad as she had expected.

But under the clothes, she was sweating like crazy and she knew she needed more water pretty quickly and to get cooled down. And from the looks of Colfax, he did as well.

They went into the Institute, up the flight of stairs in case any of the local staff was around, and then through a secret panel in the wall of her room.

A few minutes later she was stripping out of the hat and gloves and long-sleeved blouse in the coolness of the cavern.

Colfax went right to the kitchen area and got them large glasses of cold water, which they both drank completely. Then he refilled both glasses and set them on the table and took off his suit jacket.

She turned and asked him to unbutton her dress.

"That was hot," she said.

"Why we left so early," he said. "You got to be really careful with water and such if you travel during the day on these western summer days."

She understood that now completely. So much about this time period that she had to learn. And dying from heat stroke wasn't one of the things she wanted to experience.

She slipped out of the dress, leaving herself standing there only in her modern underwear and sports bra.

He took off his shirt and she was surprised at the muscles.

She reached over and took his hand. "I need a shower, you need a shower. You soap my back, I'll soap yours."

Before he could say anything, she pulled him past the kitchen area and into the back where modern showers were set up. They used the women's showers in case another traveler showed up.

An hour later they were both a lot cleaner and a lot cooler.

And they had taken the attraction to a relationship.

Anna loved every moment of that.

No doubt in her mind, 1902 was a very good year.

PART TWO
Not a Part of History

SEVEN

October 24th, 1902
Boise, Idaho

FOR COLFAX, THE last two months with Anna had been like a wonderful dream. They had spent morning, noon, and night with each other every day and he had loved every minute of it. They just seemed to fit together. And they both enjoyed the other person's passion toward their work.

Often they were working silently, sometimes they were laughing, other times they were planning on how to figure out this mystery of the Concord stagecoach.

They had stayed at the Institute, only going into Boise to get supplies a few times. And twice he had popped back to 2017 to get modern equipment and more peanut butter for the cookies.

He had learned one thing in the last few months. He never got tired of peanut butter cookies.

Now today was the day. They had decided to book a ride on the stage up to the New Meadows area, to first try to understand the route, and also what might have happened.

One theory they had was that the last run didn't have any passengers, and the owners knew it was the last run of the year, and of the business, and just ditched the stagecoach. So as paying customers, if that theory was correct, this last run before winter would get the coach left in New Meadows.

And thus change all the futures leading from these actions.

And since they were doing this in an infinite number of timelines, their very investigation might be the cause of the two different outcomes. Bonnie and Duster had done math on that sort of thing, from what Anna had told him. They believed that might be possible.

But she stressed that nothing was for sure.

Anna told him that she had a hunch on this one. She thought they were going to be right.

The day before, Colfax and Anna had gone into Boise and he had rented a suite there at the Idanha Hotel for a month for the two of them, posing as husband and wife. They would leave their horses there in the stable for the time they would be gone.

The morning was bitingly cold and smelled like snow to Colfax. He and Anna had bundled up and left the hotel even too early for breakfast. They had some food and survival gear in their luggage, enough to last them for a week if they watched it.

Both of them wore layers, including thermal underwear designed in 2117 to look like the underwear worn in this time period. Both of them actually had on two pairs of gloves and two pairs of socks. The weather, they knew, for this day, would be cold and it would be snowing by the time they reached the New Meadows area in two days.

Colfax had rented them a carriage to take them out to the stage line start and Anna was surprised at how rough the ride was.

"Just wait until you are in the coach," Colfax had said. "I hear they are worse."

He had never ridden in a stagecoach, which surprised even himself when she asked him that question. He had always just preferred horses or trains for longer trips.

As they neared the place, the sun was just coming up and Anna gasped when they rounded some trees and could see the big stagecoach sitting in front of the shack, four horses harnessed up and waiting.

Actually, he gasped as well.

From a historical perspective, the Concord stage had a mythic quality about it. The classic egg-shape with a flat roof with rails that allowed people to sit up there. The three windows on the side that were covered in leather pull-down curtains to try to keep out the dust. The smaller front wheels, larger back wheels, and the leather baggage area on the back.

To Colfax, these coaches represented much of what he found special about the Old West.

In their days, the Concords were the best coaches made and were very expensive. In the years before the railroad, they were the only transportation across the country besides walking or riding a horse.

That time hadn't lasted that long, from the Oregon Trail to the transcontinental railroad, but in those couple of generations, the big Concords were the top of the line.

As the carriage dropped them off and the driver sat their bags beside the Concord, Colfax was stunned at the size of the thing. He had been close and even sat in a Concord Coach before, but he had forgotten how tall and large they actually were. Amazing four horses could pull it.

As he looked closer, he could see a lot of wear on the coach. Some of the polished wood and much of the painted wood had been scraped and one of the leather curtains was tattered.

Some areas were worn more than others, clearly from people climbing on and off.

Even in its majesty, the poor thing just looked old and tired. There was an old saying about Concords: They never broke down, they just wore out.

Anna was just staring up at it like she had seen a ghost.

He touched her shoulder gently. "You all right?"

She nodded. "Just surprised that this one stagecoach and this one run could change so much of this planet's future. It seems larger than life."

He laughed. "It is actually large."

With that he walked around the coach and knocked on the shed door.

"Come on in," a man's voice said.

Colfax opened the door and held it for Anna.

Inside, a potbellied stove kept the small space far too hot. The floor was wood and hadn't been swept in years and a guy with a bright smile and gray hair stood from behind a desk.

He stuck out his hand. "Jason Adams."

Colfax shook his hand and introduced Anna as if they were married.

Adams seemed a little like his coach, to have seen his better days. His hand was calloused from hard work and his arms were extra large. But he seemed nice enough.

Neither he nor Anna had found any reference to the guy after this run. Seems he just retired and lived quietly for the rest of his life.

Colfax paid Adams for the trip. Adams put the money in a small cash box and then said, "Follow me, let's get your stuff situated."

Adams put the cash box under the driver's seat in a hidden compartment there, then helped Colfax load his and Anna's bag into the back carrier and strap them in.

"One more thing to get and we can be on our way," Adams said.

He went back inside, leaving the door standing open.

Colfax watched him.

Adams checked that the fire was burning down, then put on a coat and hat and gloves, then grabbed two clearly heavy satchels from beside his desk.

He brought them out, clearly struggling with the weight.

"Need help with those?" Colfax asked, glancing at Anna who was looking puzzled.

"Just open the stage door if you would," Adams said.

Colfax had to step up to pull open the stage door, the heavy leather curtains flapping.

Adams tossed the two bags on the floor of the large passenger compartment, then climbed up and raised up the front bench seat and put both of the heavy bags under the seat, then snapped it closed and locked it with a padlock.

"Mail and other deliveries," he said, smiling. "Helps pay the costs."

"I can understand that," Colfax said.

Adams offered his hand to Anna to help her up and into the coach.

Then Colfax followed.

The inside had a lot more room than he had imagined. He couldn't stand up, but he bet Anna could.

He sat next to Anna on the back bench seat, facing forward. She had a stunned look on her face.

"First stop in about two hours," Adams said, looking in at them from ground.

With that he closed the door on them, plunging them into almost total blackness behind the leather dust curtains.

"Oh, shit," Anna said. "What are we doing?"

"Just taking a ride is all," Colfax said, putting his hand on her leg, then moving to lift one of the leather curtains so they had some light.

"I hope you are right," Anna said, the worry in her voice clear.

And he was worried as well, but not so much about what might happen, but about the rough ride they were going to have to endure for three days.

Just as he got the curtain up and tied, Adams climbed up on the driver's seat, rocking the entire stage.

And a moment later they were moving.

And within a hundred yards, Colfax knew his worry was real. And why he'd never been in a stage before as he and Anna scrambled to find something to hold onto to keep from sliding and tumbling all over the couch. And they hadn't even left the mostly flat valley floor. He had no idea what this was going to be like in the mountains.

And thank heavens he had opened the window, even though the wind coming through was bitingly cold. The descriptions of the rocking on the large leather shock absorbers didn't do the reality justice.

He had been on smoother ships on rough seas.

A few moments later, Anna said, "Who knew you would need Dramamine in a stage coach."

She scrambled to the open window and lost what little breakfast they had eaten.

As soon as she was done, he did the same.

This was going to be a very, very long trip.

EIGHT

October 24th, 1902
Boise, Idaho

ONE LONG HOUR and seventeen minutes after they started, the rocking and bouncing and jerking of the coach came to a stop.

Anna had her head tucked against Colfax and they had been braced against each other for the last hour after the rocking cost them both their breakfasts.

She glanced at her watch and looked up at him.

Colfax now looked worried. That was not a look on him she had been used to.

He pointed up the brush and scrub-tree covered hill they could see outside the coach from the one window they had left open.

"That's where they find the coach," he said softly. "I spent a lot of time out here and standing on this old road looking up as the crews dug up this coach."

"Oh, shit," Anna said. "We need to get out of here and now."

It hadn't dawned on either one of them that they might need a gun. Stagecoach robberies by 1902 were almost a thing of the past.

As Colfax reached for the door, it jerked open.

They were facing a man with a thick black beard, uncut black hair, a heavy-looking long leather coat, and an old revolver in his hand pointing at them.

"Time to stretch your legs," the man said.

He stepped back as Colfax climbed down, then helped Anna down. She looked into Colfax's eyes and didn't see any fear, even though she was so afraid she could hardly move.

And both of her hands were shaking.

The man indicated they should go around behind the coach and stand on the road.

He made them walk ten steps and then stop and turn to face him.

Colfax had his arm around her.

Anna worked to take a deep breath, to get her wits about her.

The day around them was gray and dark and a light snow was starting to fall. Most of the trees had lost their leaves and below them a ways was the Boise River, its cold-looking dark water twisting through the valley.

Colfax just squeezed her shoulders to tell her it would be all right. She knew he had spent almost eight hundred years back in this time. He understood it.

Thank heavens he was here with her. She was so far out of her knowledge depth it wasn't even funny.

At that moment another man came from around the front of the stage with a pistol pointing in the back of Adams.

The other robber also had a long black beard and a long coat and cowboy boots. He had on a cowboy hat that looked more from Texas than here in the west and he had it tied under his chin with a leather strap.

He was also carrying the cash box that Adams had stashed under his seat.

As she and Colfax watched, the robbers forced Adams, who was saying nothing, to climb into the coach and open the lock on the seat inside and get out the two heavy bags.

Adams dropped them on the ground, then climbed down.

Before Anna had a chance to breathe, the second man shot Adams in the chest without even a word.

The sound was louder than anything Anna could have ever imagined and she and Colfax jerked backwards.

The man shot Adams again, this time in the head, as he lay on the ground.

At that moment, Anna knew she and Colfax were going to die.

"Wait for me on the other side," Colfax whispered.

Anna nodded.

"Who are you men?" Colfax asked, stepping slightly forward to be in front of her. "Stagecoach robberies ended years ago."

The guy who had shot Adams laughed and picked up the bags. "Just a couple of brothers looking to buy a ranch."

"And with what you two have in your pockets and luggage," the man in front of them said, "me and Billy just might have enough."

With that the man in front of Colfax shot him squarely in the chest.

The noise was so loud, it again stunned Anna as Colfax slumped to the ground.

Anna looked down at the man she had come to love in the last two months, lying in the dirt, bleeding.

Then she got angry.

Really angry.

Uncontrolled anger.

She screamed and ran at the man with the gun.

There was a loud noise and she found herself standing in the crystal cavern under the Institute, touching the wooden box.

Only two minutes and fifteen seconds had passed since she had left 2017 to jump back to 1902.

Around her the narrow hallway-like cavern had thousands of crystals, all representing different timelines, in small niches in the rock. They all glowed a faint pink with energy.

The narrow cavern was over a hundred yards long and had crystals every foot along the way and five high.

A wire fence from floor to ceiling protected the crystals and wooden tables with wooden boxes on them stretched the entire length down the middle.

The wooden boxes were the invention that Bonnie and Duster had come up with to allow them to go back in time in other timelines.

She had gone about halfway down and picked a crystal in the middle of a group in the middle row. She had hooked the two cables to it as Duster and Bonnie had shown her how to do a very long time ago now.

Then she had set the target time she wanted to jump to on the wooden box on the wooden table in the middle of the narrow cavern. Then she had hooked up the two wires and found herself in 1902.

Right now the two wires were still hooked up to the crystal and the box. Only she had died in that timeline and was now back here, where she started, just a few minutes later.

She had been shot. In a stagecoach robbery of all things.

Her knees and hands were shaking so hard she couldn't control them. She slumped to the rock floor of the narrow cavern, resting her back against the wooden leg of the table.

That was the first time in over a thousand years of living and traveling in both the past and her future that she had died.

She knew many travelers had died, most just from staying in a timeline and dying of old age or some disease. She had known that in theory, but never had it happen to her before now.

She had always moved around through time and timelines so much, dying had never been an issue.

And dying violently was something she had never imagined.

She looked over at the wall with the crystal with the cords attached to it. In that timeline and in an infinite number of them, she had been gunned down in 1902.

She did the math on all this, understood the numbers, but now for the first time, was starting to understand the real people and events behind all her math.

And wow did that make a massive difference.

She sat there taking deep breaths until she finally got her nerves calmed down enough to take off her heavy winter gloves and put on a protective glove and unhook the wires from the box and the crystal.

Then on the clipboard under the crystal, she marked her name, the time she was there, and made a notation as to the robbery.

Then she headed down the long room, taking off her outer coat as she went.

Beyond the long crystal room was another long hallway with upwards of a hundred doors along one side. Each door had a crystal room just like the one she had been in.

Each crystal had been brought here from what Duster and Bonnie called the nexus, where all time and energy combine into a physical form in the crystal.

Bonnie and Duster had proven mathematically that all time, energy, and matter were connected.

Each time there is a decision by anyone, a new crystal and timeline is formed. The nexus is basically an infinitely large location for the combination of time and energy in its matter form.

She hoped to have Bonnie and Duster take her to see it some time. So far she hadn't asked.

As she walked down the hallway toward the large cavern of supplies for the Old West, she thought about how brave and calm Colfax had been. He understood the Old West and he got information from their killers that would help them.

But she had a problem. He didn't leave here in 2017 for two more days yet.

She would see how much research she could find on those brothers before he got back.

And she would have to make sure she didn't run into him in any way when he came through to go back to 1902. They would be synced up when he returned.

And she could hardly wait. She was already missing him.

And that surprised her more than she wanted to admit.

NINE

September 4th, 2017
Boise, Idaho

COLFAX STEPPED BACK away from the wooden box and took a deep breath. No way a person could ever get used to dying suddenly. He felt as if every nerve in his body was firing at the same time.

And his stomach from that coach ride still felt like it had spent far too long on the open seas in a small fishing boat.

He had died five times before this in the Old West. Twice from old age, twice from rock slides, once from drowning in a flash flood, and now the sixth time he was shot in a stagecoach robbery.

He sure hoped Anna was all right. Often women didn't get the easy way out of situations like that. His only hope was that she charged them and made them kill her quickly.

Or that she had some self-defense experience she hadn't told him about. That more than likely would be the case. They had so much to learn about each other.

Dying in the past had just never been anything either of them had thought to talk about. In fact, he had never told her he had died a number of times and he had never asked if she had.

He took a deep breath to not only calm his nerves, but to settle his stomach a little more.

Then he unhooked the wires from the box, then took the wires off the crystal and wrote on the clipboard what had happened.

Then he headed toward the supply room to ditch his layers of clothes and put on some 2017 clothes.

Ten minutes later he cleared the stairs and went into the big cavern. His stomach was still twisting from the stage ride, but his nerves from being shot were a lot calmer.

Bonnie and Duster were still sitting at the kitchen counter and Anna was standing behind the counter. And the smell of peanut butter cookies filled the air like a welcoming blanket on a cold night.

Just as it had done when he had left the cavern fifteen minutes before. Of course. But this time he knew what that smell meant.

She beamed when she saw him and ran and gave him a massive hug and kiss.

"Told you to watch out for her, didn't I?" Duster said, laughing.

Colfax just shook his head. Of course they knew what was going to happen

More Thunder Mountain Novels
Available at your favorite booksellers.

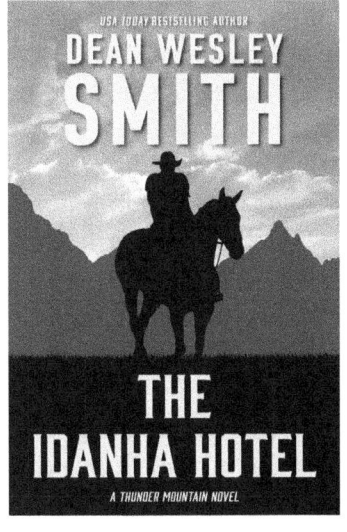
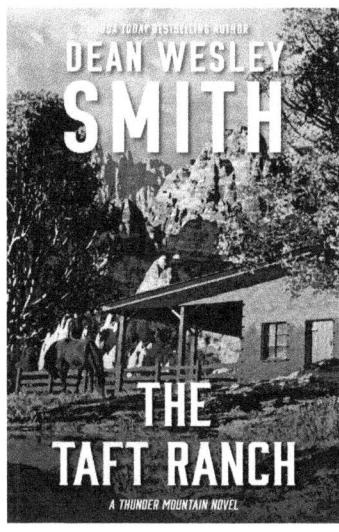

when he left, but couldn't say a word to him about it.

Sometimes time travel just confused the hell out of him. But he was very grateful that dying in another timeline wasn't fatal in this one.

After he kissed Anna another time, he looked into her eyes, "Are you all right?"

"First time on the death stuff for me," she said. "But past that, yes. I was so angry that they shot you that I attacked them like an out-of-control red-haired lioness and they had to shoot me as well."

"Very smart thinking," he said, laughing.

"That's what Bonnie said. Only I wasn't thinking. Seeing you lying there bleeding just made me angry. I don't know for sure, but I hope I got in a few kicks before they shut me down."

He hugged her and kissed her again.

"Thank you," he said.

"Thank you for having the presence of mind to get information from them."

"They figure dead people don't talk," he said, smiling at her.

"If they only knew."

They both laughed and turned back to Bonnie and Duster.

"I made you a bowl of chicken soup," Anna said, indicating he should sit at the counter. "It was all my stomach could handle after that ride and shock of dying."

"Sounds wonderful," he said.

He glanced at Bonnie and Duster. "You ever ride in a stage?"

"Once," they both said at the same time.

Colfax laughed. "A little warning might have been nice."

"You wouldn't have believed us if we did warn you away from those things," Duster said. "Those coaches were all hype and ugly reality."

"Yeah, I think we got our 'once' in as well," Anna said as she slid the soup in front of Colfax.

"And don't forget to give him a peanut butter cookie," Duster said. "This woman has been killing all of us here for the past two days with those damned things."

Colfax laughed. "If you got to go, I can think of worse ways."

At that Bonnie laughed and Duster just smiled and nodded.

"I got a fresh batch in the cabinet," Anna said, smiling at Duster.

So as Colfax sipped on the soup, Anna told them all about her research over the last few days while waiting for him.

"The jerks who shot us were Billy and Danny Thorpe," she said. "They were never caught and the robbery was never reported, which is why that coach being up there was such a mystery."

"No idea what was in those bags?" Colfax asked.

"Not a clue anywhere," Anna said.

Colfax sipped on the wonderful tasting chicken noodle soup while she talked.

"About six months after the robbery, they bought a large ranch on the main road to Emmett, on a rise. The ranch is still there, passed down through their family. A pretty large spread."

He glanced up at her and could see the worry in her eyes. "I am sensing a problem you haven't told me about just yet."

Duster and Bonnie both laughed.

Anna just smiled that fond smile at him that in two months together he had come to really love.

"I jumped to my time and then to 2217," she said. "The Thorpe family ends up helping to build some hospitals with their money and two of them through the two centuries end up as pretty powerful Senators."

"You have got to be kidding me?" Colfax couldn't believe what he had just heard.

She shook her head. "I'm not."

His stomach had just begun to settle when she said that. Now it was all twisted back up again.

"So we go back and stop the robbery, we get a future with anti-gravity. We don't stop it and we got hospitals and a family that does good through the years. Right?"

"Nothing is for certain in time travel," Bonnie said. "Remember that."

Colfax nodded.

"And we don't know the ramifications of whatever is in those bags getting through to the people or person expecting them," Anna said.

He looked into her worried green eyes.

"Does math tell us what to do in this case?" he asked.

Duster and Bonnie both laughed at that.

And he honestly had no idea why that was even funny.

TEN

September 5th, 2017
Boise, Idaho

COLFAX AND ANNA stood on the old road, about in the same position they had stood in 1902 when they were shot. Just around the corner, the old road crossed over Dry Creek. Actually, the old road went down through the creek bed.

There was very little left of this old road. More of just a flat area cut out of the hill now covered in tall weeds and a few scrub trees.

He had only been back a day, but he was feeling almost normal now. They had decided to get out here early to see what they could find while their memories were fresh.

Around them, the day was going to be hot. It was only nine in the morning and they could feel it starting to heat up. Not at all like the last time when they had stood here in the cold and lightly blowing snow.

Both Anna and Colfax had worn high-topped leather boots, leathers under the jeans up to their knees, and then jeans. Colfax's crew from the historical society had constantly had to deal with rattlers in this area. No point in getting sick if one of the snakes got a bite in. Not deadly, but not fun either.

Both of them had on thin shirts and wide-brimmed hats. He hated getting sunburned as much as she did.

He had three of his crew with him, just now pulling up behind the Institute's Cadillac SUV in a white van.

"So we figured out how they got the stage up there," Colfax said. "They took it around the corner and up the gully and over that ridge. Then they unhooked the horses and pushed the Concord down into that deep canyon."

Anna nodded. "But I want to know what they did with our bodies. Or at least Adams' body. Since the stage was found up there, a body needs to be around somewhere."

"Let's assume," Colfax said, "that even though we might not have been in this timeline with the stage, they shot Adams in the same spot."

He stopped and looked around. "You wouldn't drag a body uphill and you wouldn't bother to put it in the stage. Besides, when we dug up the stage, there was no body in it."

They both walked through the weeds growing up on the old dirt road and looked down toward the valley below. About thirty paces down the steep hill was a small rock outcropping that hid the bottom of the rock cliff.

"They rolled Adams, and maybe us over the cliff," Anna said.

Colfax agreed. "That's why they stopped the stage right here, because of that hiding spot. They planned on killing everyone in the stage."

Colfax waved his crew of two college-aged girls and a college-aged boy over and pointed downward. They were grad students in history at the University and were interning at the Historical Society.

All three were experts in archeological digs and knew what to touch, how to dig, and when to stop.

He pointed at the rock outcropping below them. "Going to be a lot of snakes so be really careful." All three of them shrugged. "But we need to see what is at the bottom of that little rock outcropping."

With shovels in hand, they started down the hill.

"Shout if you find signs of anything at all," he said.

"Sure thing, Director," one of them said.

Anna and Colfax watched, standing in the hot sun, as it took the students a good ten minutes to pick their way down the steep hill and around the small rock outcropping. A couple times they batted at snakes along the way, but clearly those three had no fear or worry about snakes at all.

All three of them disappeared below the rocks.

"You can't see anything from up here and nothing from there could be seen from below," Anna said. "Perfect spot."

Colfax nodded and they waited in the warming morning air.

"Dr. Shaw," one of the kids shouted, his voice echoing. "You might want to take a look at this."

He glanced at Anna. "You ready for a climb?"

"Ever tell you I hate snakes?" she said.

"No issue, stay here," he said.

"Not a chance," she said, laughing.

"We're coming!" Colfax shouted down to his crew.

Then carefully, he and Anna followed the path the students had gone, luckily without seeing a snake at all.

They got around to the lower part of the cliff and all three students were standing off to one side, staring at a long crevice in the rocks. All three of them looked shocked, actually.

One of them pointed and Anna and Colfax went over to get a closer look.

There, tucked back in the rocks, were three skeletons. Their heavy coats and clothing mostly tatters. A couple of snakes were curled up in the bones, rattling a warning at the intrusion.

"Okay, we're done here," Colfax said as he and Anna stepped back from the rocks.

"Did you know they were going to be there?" one student asked.

"No driver for that coach up there, and no robbery reported in history, so that gave a good chance a body was around here somewhere," Colfax said. "Just logical follow-the-clues thinking."

All three students nodded as he pulled out his cell phone and called the Institute and got through to Director Parks. "Need to get the police and others out here. We found three bodies."

"Yours and Anna's?" he asked.

"Without a doubt," Colfax said.

"Understood," Parks said.

Anna looked puzzled as Colfax hung up.

He would explain to her later that finding modern underwear and stuff on two bodies from 1902 always caused problems. So Parks had a couple people on staff that took care of such strange details and made sure none of the modern stuff got to any report.

The three grad students were already halfway back up the hill when Anna took one more look at the bodies, then shook her head.

"Really strange to know that's me in there."

"It's not, really, is it?" Colfax asked.

"No, it's not. It's me from another timeline."

"And our bodies, these bodies, are being found in yet another timeline. Right?"

"Actually two timelines," she said, smiling at him. "You were in one and I was in another, remember?"

"You mean the woman I had wild sex with for two months wasn't you?" Colfax asked, laughing.

"Technically, no, it wasn't," she said, smiling. "Just as technically, those aren't my bones in those rocks there."

"But last night was really you?" he asked.

"That was all me," she said. "And I'll show you even more of that later if you get me out of this snake pit."

"With pleasure," he said. He led the way up the hill, with her holding onto the belt in the back of his pants and staying very close to him as a snake guard.

Then they went and sat in the Cadillac with the air-conditioning running to drink water and wait for the police.

After a few minutes, Anna shook her head and giggled.

He glanced over at her and she was just shaking her head. "I just realized I am sitting here, waiting for the police to come to my murder scene so I can show them where my body is."

"And you are not a ghost," he said.

They both laughed, then she said, "Nope, nothing weird about this at all."

"Happens every day," he said.

"Damn I hope not," she said.

And with that he had to agree with her completely.

ELEVEN

September 10th, 2017
Boise, Idaho

ANNA SPENT THE next five nights with Colfax in his Institute condo. She had one in this timeline as well, but his was furnished and had food and supplies. She hadn't taken the time yet in 2017 to do anything with hers. It had just been sort of like a hotel room she had used a few times over the last year.

Her real condo was a hundred years in the future. That one she had fixed up, spent time and energy making it hers.

She really liked Colfax's place. He had made it comfortable and it only took a little extra to give her an office in the spare bedroom and some high-speed computers attached to the Institute computers.

She liked being in his place, waking up next to him in the morning, talking about history and timelines with him. Never before in her life had she been lucky enough to find someone like him.

And thankfully, he liked her as well.

They had spent the five days searching for even more about what would happen if Jason Adams lived, if the two brothers didn't buy their ranch, and so on.

History gave them no clear answers and the future outcomes over the next few hundred years just complicated everything.

Plus, as Duster had said two days ago when they were talking with him and Bonnie, "History doesn't require you to do anything you know. Or job is to study history, not try to fix it."

And that simple statement worried her more than she wanted to admit.

History really didn't require them to do anything but study it.

Right now, from her research and calculations and explorations into other future timelines, the anti-gravity was in a great many timelines. In a great many histories, the brothers do not rob that stage and kill the driver.

But as Colfax asked her last night, does that happen because the two of them go back and do something, or is that a natural happening?

And they had no way of finding that out.

They, as observers, might even have changed the timeline. That question alone on this would take a decade of math and computer time to figure out.

So on the sixth morning, Colfax said, "Ready to go back again?"

She had known that was coming, but honestly, it scared her to death. It was a different world, 1902.

"Not really," she said. "But I think if we're going to learn more, we need to."

"I agree," he said.

"But no more riding in stagecoaches," she said.

"Never," he said, laughing.

So they walked hand in hand along the Greenbelt path that skirted the river to the Institute, enjoying the fall morning. It was still warm and the leaves hadn't started to turn yet. But that wasn't far off.

She loved this time of year.

There was no one in the cavern when they got there and they went right on through and down to the supply room for 1902. They went to a different crystal and set the date for October 10th, 1902. They would not run into

themselves because by going back there, an infinite number of timelines split off that they were not present in.

Again, with her math, things like that would have to be accounted for.

By the time they got back up to the big empty cavern in 1902, her nerves were shot.

The big cavern had a fire going in the fireplace, but it felt empty.

"We need some cookies," Colfax said, unpacking the jars of peanut butter and supplies they had brought from the future on the big wooden table. "You cook, I'll carry stuff upstairs to our room."

"Deal," she said, laughing.

He was right, the fresh smell of cookies would really help this place and calm her down. In just a few months it seemed he knew her better than she knew herself at times.

As Colfax set up their computers in the couch and chair area in front of the fireplace and then left with their bags of clothing to take them upstairs into the mansion, she got the stove going and got the cookies mixed.

By the time he came back down, the large cavern smelled heavenly.

"There is nothing better to make a place smell like home than fresh cookies," he said, coming across the room to sit at the kitchen table to talk with her.

"Why real estate agents through the years bake cookies or fresh bread before open houses," she said.

"And there's a job I know nothing about," he said. "Never owned a piece of property."

She smiled at him. "I never have either. Never found one I wanted enough to buy, actually."

"Bonnie and Duster take you up to the Monumental Summit Lodge?"

"No, why?" she asked.

"That's a place you would want, I am sure," he said, laughing. "When we get back we can go see it and I'll tell you some of the stories about the place."

She liked the sound of that.

Ten minutes later, with a plate of hot peanut butter cookies on the coffee table between them, they sat in front of the fire in the stone fireplace and tried to work out what they wanted to do.

She had no idea what to do next. But she had a hunch that the two of them could figure it out.

PART THREE
Not Mathematically Possible

TWELVE

October 24th, 1902
Boise, Idaho

COLFAX COULD NOT believe how cold the morning was. He remembered it being cold the last time, but not this cold. Of course, they had been forced to ride out along the Boise River trail, basically the remains of the old Oregon Trail, just as the sun came up enough to see.

That ride had been cold, much colder than being in the rocking stage because of the wind. Even with a heavy coat and two pairs of gloves, his hands felt like blocks of ice and he had lost touch with his feet a half hour before.

They had brought high-powered cameras with long-range lenses with them from the future. They planned on watching and photographing the event of the robbery.

What they had figured out over the last few weeks of planning was that they had no plan. They had solved the riddle of how the Concord Coach had gotten up in that gulley.

And Anna had solved the riddle of why sometimes the coach didn't end up in a New Meadow's barn to change a kid's life in the future.

But what they didn't know was what event triggered the coach to make it all the way through to New Meadows. What event stopped the robbery?

So they had decided to come out here, watch from a distance with high-powered lenses and cameras, and then go back to 2017 to try to figure it out, trace events leading up to the stage ride.

The morning air had a sharp wind that cut at them and light flakes of snow were drifting through the air, not enough yet to cause visibility problems, thankfully.

They both had double coats, modern thermal underwear, and double gloves and hats. The wind still cut through it all.

They got into position under some tall pines that gave them an unobstructed view of the corner where the robbery would take place. The only sounds around them were the wind in the trees and the river bubbling around a few rocks just downstream from where they were.

He got his scope and camera set up on a tripod just fine, even with frozen fingers, and focused in on the hillside.

"Set here," he said.

"Also here," she said.

He glanced at his watch. "Ten minutes."

She nodded, jumping up and down a little to try to get a little warmer. He

wasn't sure he wanted to try that. He was afraid his frozen feet would shatter.

"Here come the brothers," Anna whispered.

He turned to see that the two brothers were riding up the trail in the opposite direction from where the stage would be coming. When they got to where the trail crossed over Dry Creek, they tied up their horses and kept going on foot.

From what Colfax could see, the cold didn't seem to be bothering them in the slightest.

"Stage," Anna whispered.

Colfax's stomach twisted as he turned to his camera.

He could see the brother's faces clearly and both of them had their hands on their guns sticking out of their belts.

The stage came into sight and the brothers took out their guns.

Adams slowed the stage and stopped as he had done when they were inside.

Colfax made sure his camera was recording everything, then he whispered to Anna, "Are you sure there is no chance we're going to climb out of that stage?"

She laughed. "Thankfully, yes, I am one hundred percent sure. And that one I can explain with math if you want me to try later in front of a warm fire."

"Oh, good," he said. "Didn't want to watch myself get killed."

"Luckily, with the rules of these timelines and how the math works, those kinds of ugly time loops can't happen."

He actually felt thankful for that.

Adams was behind the large coach when suddenly a shot echoed over the valley. Then another.

A moment later one of the brothers dragged Adam's body around the back of the coach and off the edge of the road, rolling it down toward the outcropping of rocks below.

The brother followed the rolling body until it stopped, then took it around the rocks and stuffed it into the crevice.

In the meantime, the other brother had gotten the stage moving again and took it on around the corner to where they had tied their horses, then up a steep embankment, pushing the horses hard to pull it up.

After the first brother took care of the body, he climbed back up and went up the hill to help unhitch the coach from the horses.

Then he walked the horses back down to where their horses were and tied them up. Then he grabbed two shovels and went back to the coach.

The other brother searched every inch of the big coach and when his brother got back, together they managed to get it rolling and shove it over the edge.

The sound of the coach crashing into the narrow canyon echoed over the river.

Then both went down the steep slope and started shoving dirt from the hillside down on the wreckage.

And they cut off some brush and piled it on the lower side so no one from the road could see it.

"This was very well planned out," Anna said as the two brothers finished and went down the gulley to the road and then back around to their horses and the stage horses.

Colfax had to agree with that. Very well planned out.

So now they had all the images of exactly what happened that they would need to study.

And nowhere in anything they had seen did he see a way that Concord Coach ended up in that barn in New Meadows. Nowhere.

They were missing something.

Something big.

THIRTEEN

September 17th, 2017
Boise, Idaho

THE SMELL OF garlic-buttered breadsticks filled the air of the Brooks Garden restaurant and the light sounds of other patrons talking felt like comforting background noise.

The Brooks Garden was one of those Italian restaurants that divided every table or booth with plants. Lush plants that seemed to grow toward the high ceilings, even in the dim light.

Anna and Colfax were seated in the back in a large booth completely surrounded on three sides by plants. Anna was sure it would take a guide to get them back to the front door through the jungle maze. But she liked it here, not only for the soft, garlic breadsticks that melted in her mouth, but because talking was private.

Colfax and Anna often ate dinner here a few times a week. A lot of the people from the Institute did, actually. It wouldn't have surprised Anna at all if Bonnie and Duster owned part of this place.

This had been Colfax's idea to go out for lunch, since she was getting more and more frustrated with their lack of progress.

They had watched the images of that robbery over and over, looking for any detail that could be changed to change the outcome.

There was none.

Which meant that whatever changed the robbery was away from the robbery. Some time before and it must have happened either to the stage, to Adams, or the brothers. Millions of possibilities.

So they had gone back through the records, looking at events that might have caused that coach ride that day to not happen.

There was none.

Jason Adams was going to take that ride one way or another and die that day.

Yet somehow, some way, that Concorde Coach ended up in a barn in New Meadows in some timelines. Not all, but some.

The lunch rush of office workers in the downtown area needing to go back to work had just finished when they got there, so they managed to get their favorite booth clear in the back.

"So," Colfax said after the waiter brought them both iced teas and glasses of water and a second basket of breadsticks. "We have an impossible occurrence."

She nodded.

"But we know it can't be impossible. There has to be an answer."

They had walked the mile or so from the Institute to the restaurant and the day was warming up. Not summer warm, but a nice fall day warm that still heated them up.

After that morning by the river taking pictures of the robbery, any kind of warmth pleased Anna at this point. But she still took a long drink of water before answering Colfax.

"Exactly. It happens, so it is not impossible."

They sat silently thinking, both working on a breadstick. Anna knew she had to be careful because she could eat an entire basket of the warm, soft, wonderful-tasting garlic sticks all by herself. Just the butter on them alone had to be a billion calories.

And the waiter who knew them had already brought them a second basket because they always asked for more.

But what the hell. At the moment she was so frustrated, she didn't care.

Suddenly Colfax sat back, sort of staring up into the plants around their booth. Then he said, "The Concorde Coach from the New Meadows barn is in the Idaho Historical Society in some timelines, right?"

She nodded.

"Could you jump to one of those timelines and get pictures and data off that coach?"

"Sure, why?" she asked.

"Because," he said, looking at her with those fantastic brown eyes. "We have an impossible situation. The coach that we found on that hill seems to have no reason to make it all the way to New Meadows."

Suddenly she realized where he was headed. "You think the New Meadows coach might be a different Concord Coach?"

"Only one way to find out," he said, smiling and nodding. "You jump to get the data from another timeline on the one from New Meadows and I'll get the interns and myself putting that coach we found up in the ravine back together. As much as possible, that is."

She scooted quickly around in the booth and kissed him hard and long.

"Oh, my," he said after she let him come up for air. "What was that for?"

"For bringing me to this wonderful restaurant," she said, munching on another garlic bread stick and smiling at him.

He held up a bread stick and pretended to study it. "If these get that kind of reaction, I got to get their recipe."

She laughed and that felt wonderful, after the last days of frustration. Finally they had a way that the impossible might be possible.

It might not pan out, but it sure seemed like it was possible and at the moment, that was all she needed.

FOURTEEN

September 17th, 2017
Boise, Idaho

AFTER THEY WALKED back from lunch, Anna headed for the crystal room and Colfax said he would wait for her in the cavern. She was going to jump to her time first, do some research for a few days on the powerful computers there, then jump to another timeline

that had the Concord Coach from New Meadows in the Historical Society, then come back.

For her, she would be gone a few days. But here she would actually be gone for just a few minutes, since she would time her arrival back to just after when she'd left so he didn't have to wait too long.

When she got back she kissed him hard again, then said, "I missed you, you know that?"

"Glad you did," he said, smiling and hugging her back. "How long were you out?"

"Three days and nights my time," she said. She patted the computer she had taken and brought back with her. "I had the computers in my time do a search of all Concord Coaches that were known to have existed and their final locations."

"How many could they track?" This actually had him excited.

"We know where just about half of the ones manufactured ended up," she said.

That number surprised him. "Only half?"

That left a lot of Concord Coaches unaccounted for.

She nodded. "And actually there is no real idea how many were made. They did seven hundred before the first time the company was restructured. Past that no real idea how many more. Records of the Abbot Downing Company in both of its incarnations don't seem to have made it into public records."

He nodded. This was starting to feel a lot more impossible, but yet likely, since there were so many coaches out there.

"I also discovered that each coach was individually numbered at the factory," she said, smiling. "The one sitting in the Idaho Historical Society in the other timeline that came out of the New Meadows barn is number four-hundred-and-seventeen."

"So let's go see if we can get an idea of what number the one we rode in is," he said.

They headed out and twenty minutes later were standing in a back room of the Idaho Historical Society.

The paved floor of the room was littered in stagecoach parts. It looked like a large model kit. And most of the parts had already been cleaned.

Colfax had five interns from the university all working on the coach project. It turned out that a lot of the buried parts were in very good shape.

Greg, the lead intern and one of the best young historians he knew, saw them and came over. He stood almost as tall as Colfax and weighed even less, if that was possible. He had dark black hair that seemed to always stand up at odd angles and dark eyes that lit up when he smiled.

"We think we can put this completely back together," Greg said.

There was clear excitement in his voice.

A couple of the others nodded without looking up from what they were doing. To them this was fantastic fun, and actually, if Colfax hadn't been so consumed with discovering the puzzle of the two coaches, he would have been in here on the floor helping them.

"We're going to need to replace some of the broken sections, mill a few others, and get new leather and such for the windows and seat cushions," Greg said. "But when we are done it will look as good as the day it ended up in that gulch."

"More than likely better," Colfax said.

Beside him Anna was nodding.

"So did you find a number on this one yet?" Anna asked.

"Sure did," Greg said, smiling. "Number four-hundred-and-seventeen of the original seven hundred they built."

Colfax just stood there, stunned.

Completely stunned.

The same number.

The exact same number.

Anna just shook her head.

"Director," Greg said. "If you wouldn't mind, we have a lead on an old Concord Coach up in New Meadows that's been sitting in a barn. We might be able to salvage some parts off of it to help with this."

Anna looked up.

"There's a coach in New Meadows?"

Greg nodded. "Some kid a while back tried to restore it, but it's in really bad shape now from what I understand. We could probably get them to give it to us as a donation, just to haul it away."

Colfax just looked at Greg, his mouth open.

So he had been right.

There were two coaches. Just not in the way he had thought.

And he had no idea what that meant at this point at all.

Not a clue.

"Greg, let Anna and me head up to New Meadows to take a look at the coach," Colfax said. "You guys keep working and I'll call you if you need to bring the truck."

"Perfect," Greg said, turning back to work with a smile. "Have fun."

Colfax took Anna's hand and they turned and left.

All the way back to the Institute they rode in silence. Neither one of them had any idea what to do now.

This had just gotten even more twisted.

And they clearly had been looking completely in the wrong place.

FIFTEEN

September 17th, 2017
Boise, Idaho

ANNA DROPPED ONTO the couch in front of the unlit fireplace in the large cavern under the Institute mansion. Colfax went over to the kitchen area and brought the plate of peanut butter cookies back to her and offered her one, which she took with a nod.

She was feeling numb, all the way to her core. Her basic assumptions had clearly been off somewhere.

He took a cookie, set the plate down on the wooden coffee table between them, and stretched out on a couch in such a way that he could see her.

They sat in silence, she trying to put her mind back together enough to even figure out where to start.

"So tell me if I am wrong," Colfax said. "The theory was that Ryder Marks loved working on the old Concord so much, he ended up going to college. Right?"

She nodded. That was her theory until today. Clearly wrong somewhere.

"But it seems that he worked on the Concord in some timelines and went to college and in other timelines he worked on the Concord and didn't go to college. Right?"

"Sure appears that way," she said. She took a bite of the cookie and closed her eyes. How could all of that math and research have been so wrong? It didn't seem possible.

"And the Idaho Historical Society goes and gets the Concord that Ryder works on for parts and that becomes the story of how the Society got the restored Concord."

"Looks that way," she said again.

"So the turning point for that future isn't the coach," Colfax said, "but what exactly happened to Ryder in and around his restoring the New Meadows coach that led him to either go to college or stay on the ranch."

She finished off the cookie and nodded.

Her research had pointed her to that exact time. She had clearly made a bad assumption that it was the restoration that caused the shift. While Ryder was doing the restoration, another factor came in that either led him to college or forced him to stay on the ranch.

"So lets head to New Meadows," Colfax said, "find out in this timeline which way Ryder went, and maybe even talk with him if he's still alive."

She looked at him like he had lost a bolt. She had a ton of math to run, calculations to refigure, research to do.

"I sure can't see what it would hurt," Colfax said. "And I got to go up there anyway to see if I can get the coach that is there for the Historical Society."

She just stared at the man she had fallen in love with over the last few months. "Are you saying we should just go ask Ryder what happened?"

Colfax sat up and looked directly at Anna. "With sex and historical puzzles, I have always found the best way to an answer is to just ask directly."

It took her a moment, then she laughed. Damn him, he could make her laugh when she flat didn't want to laugh.

And this time, he had a point. A very, very good point that might help her fine-tune the math on all this far more quickly than she would otherwise.

She picked another cookie off the plate. "So tell me, Mr. Director. How did you get so damn smart and sexy at the same time?"

He looked around, pretending he was going to tell her a secret. "Oh, that comes from a lot of practice."

She threw the last half of her cookie at him, laughing, and he actually managed to catch it and put it in his mouth in one motion.

"Now you are just showing off," she said, laughing even harder.

"Can't waste a good cookie," he said.

He stood and reached out and she took his hand and he pulled her to her feet.

"You ever been to central Idaho?" he asked as he pulled her close.

"No," she said.

"Then you are in for a stunningly beautiful drive," he said.

Then he kissed her and she kissed him back and he even had enough will power to stop where they were heading with those kisses and get them packing some clothes and into a car for a trip north.

And he had been right, it was one of the most beautiful drives she had ever taken.

SIXTEEN

September 17th, 2017
Boise, Idaho

THEY STOPPED FOR a nice dinner in a small restaurant in Cascade, Idaho, about an hour-and-a-half north of Boise. All the way they had talked while Anna was on her computer connected to the Institute trying to find out as much information about Ryder Marks as she could.

Colfax was glad Ryder was still alive and at dinner Colfax called Ryder on the number Anna had found and set up an appointment to see him the next morning at ten a.m. about the Concord Coach.

Ryder seemed genuinely pleased to hear that the Idaho State Historical Society was interested in it. He said he always felt like the thing deserved better than rotting away in an old barn.

Then, while Anna worked on digging up even more on Ryder, Colfax got them a room in McCall, Idaho, about thirty minutes away.

They focused on Ryder through the entire meal and for the first ten minutes of the drive out of Cascade before they both felt they knew enough. Something had happened during the time he was trying to restore the Concord. Tomorrow, when they talked with him about the coach, they would try to dig that information out.

"So where are we staying tonight?" Anna asked as she closed her computer and sat back and enjoyed the view of the high mountain valley they were in.

This time of the year, up this high, the leaves were turning, so gold and red colors were everywhere. Not only were the tall mountains stunning, but then add in the green and red and oranges and browns of the trees and it was like driving through a painting.

Colfax loved it up here. The only place he really loved more was the Monumental Summit Lodge. But this Cascade to McCall area came in a close second.

"A place called Shore Lodge," he said. "One of the great old lodges in the country, right on the lake. It's now a major four-star resort."

"Right on the lake?" she asked. "What lake?"

"Payette Lake," he said. "A large lake surrounded by tall mountains with the little resort town of McCall on one edge. Wait until you see it."

She nodded.

He could tell she was still upset that her original research had led her wrong, or at least she thought it had. Actually the only mistake was the thinking that the Concord Coach was the direct impact. Tomorrow, with luck, they would find out what the real impact had been on Ryder Marks.

Twenty minutes later he pulled the white Cadillac SUV from the Institute under the massive log archways of the lodge entrance and handed the keys to the valet.

He and Anna both took their own luggage, since all they had were small suitcases and computers.

The massive front doors of the lodge led them into an old wooden entryway that felt like it would have been right in 1902, even though the lodge wasn't built until 1948. And the moment they climbed the stairs, the incredible view of the lake through the massive front windows made Anna go, "Wow."

The entire lobby was made of massive polished logs and the old floors felt like they were still in old saloons.

The place had a smell of wood burning in a fireplace combined with the fantastic smell of cooking steaks.

"Wait until you taste their steaks," he said, as she just sort of stared at all the details. "And they have some soaking pools to die for."

"Now this is the way I like to see the west," she said, smiling.

"Yeah, me too," he said.

Fifteen minutes later they were in their large suite overlooking the lake. It had a massive king bed, a sliding wooden door that divided the bed from a living room, and a small kitchenette. The sun was coloring the tops of the mountains, and the air had a slight chill to it, but even so they stood on their balcony and just stared.

Payette Lake could make you do that.

They changed and went down for dinner in a dining room overlooking the lake and the long dock. The tables were set with a combination of modern and Old West flare and the smell of the food was so thick it could almost be cut.

They got a table right along the window and he just stared at the lake and the long wooden dock. He had a lot of fond memories of time on that dock.

"You seem to really love it here?" she asked, staring at him.

"Childhood spent up here with my parents," he said. "Wonderful memories is all. Learned how to water ski right out there."

"This place one of the reasons you like historical studies?"

"Actually, yes," he said, smiling. "Feels like you are sitting in history here, doesn't it?"

"It does," she said, smiling. "And thanks for sharing this with me."

"Any time," he said.

SEVENTEEN

September 18th, 2017
Boise, Idaho

ANNA WAS ACTUALLY nervous the next morning by the time they'd finished breakfast, checked out, and headed north along the two-lane highway. The morning was beautiful and the dew had just left the trees and the road.

She had put on a light jacket, but she had a hunch that she wouldn't need it once the sun hit the valley floor and started to warm things up.

She had no idea why she was feeling so nervous. More than likely because she was meeting the focus of all of her research. She had put that focus on the coach, but instead, it belonged on Ryder

Marks, the person they were headed to talk with.

She made herself take deep breaths of the cool mountain air and just watch the scenery. Colfax had been so right about the stunning beauty of this McCall area. Very rugged, yet with a modern feel. She couldn't remember anywhere else she had ever been that felt that way.

The highway went past a ski resort then dropped down a narrow canyon and out into a wide valley.

"See that little town ahead?" he asked.

She could see maybe twenty or thirty buildings and not much more across open pasture land. Some modern construction homes had been built up on the foothills in the distance, but not much else.

"That's New Meadows," he said. "The Marks' ranch is north of the town along the highway."

The town ended up being as small as it looked from a distance, with the most stunning feature an old train depot. From what Colfax told her, this was as far north as an attempted north-south railway system ever got in Idaho.

Ten minutes later they turned off the highway at a large wagon wheel marking a gravel driveway and headed through rolling farm toward the trees and mountains.

The driveway looked to be about a good half mile long and as they crested a small rise they could see a tall, two-story, well-kept white farmhouse with three gray metal out-buildings and an old red hay-barn sitting on a rise about a hundred yards away.

Anna was impressed. This was a very nice ranch.

Very nice. The Marks clearly had money.

As they pulled up in front of the farmhouse and shut down the car, an older man stepped out onto the front porch.

He looked to be about sixty, with short gray hair and sunburned face and arms. He had on jeans, cowboy boots, and a plaid work shirt.

"Damn I'm scared," Anna said, under her breath.

Colfax put a hand on her leg. "He's just a regular guy who has no idea about anything in the future."

She nodded and they climbed out. Colfax's touch helped, but his words didn't.

The man came off the porch with a smile and a solid handshake as Colfax introduced himself and then Anna.

"Ryder Marks," the man said. "Great to meet you."

Anna could only nod. At the moment she didn't trust herself to talk and that, for her, was damn odd.

After chatting for a few minutes about the incredible beauty of the ranch and the entire area for a moment, Colfax got the conversation directed at the Concord Coach.

"It ain't much to look at," Ryder said, leading the way toward the big, two-story towering red barn up a slight grade. "I kept her in a back room up here, sealed up for a long time. Never really knew what to do with her."

Anna found it interesting how Ryder thought of the coach as a her. Clearly he cared about it and wanted to take care of it in a very old-fashioned way.

"Did you think about restoring the coach?" Colfax asked.

"Oh, sure," he said, "back when we first found it and Dad helped me get it up into the barn. Got a start on it."

"What stopped you?" Anna asked, managing to speak for the first time.

Ryder shrugged. "High school stuff, mostly. Made the football team as a junior and never really had time after that. A couple of my kids, when they were coming up thought about it as well. Just never hit the top of the pile for them or me, if you know what I mean."

Colfax laughed. "I sure do."

Anna just shook her head. Could it be that entire timelines and major futures changed because a high school kid in the middle of Idaho made his football team? Was that even possible?

They went into the large barn that actually felt light and open, which surprised Anna. It smelled like hay and seemed much warmer than the colder morning air outside. The large wood rafters and massive beams towered over them.

Hay in bundles was stacked on both sides of the barn up almost two stories tall. A wide walkway of hard dirt was down the middle.

Ryder went to a back wall of the barn and took a key and unlocked a large wooden-plank door, sliding it back to show the stagecoach.

Anna was surprised at how it looked. All four wheels were off and the coach itself sat up on blocks on its axles. The doors on both sides were off, as were the curtains.

The wood looked to be in great shape in most places and both she and Colfax walked around the thing, touching it like they were inspecting a used car.

"She is pretty special," Colfax said, coming back over to stand by Ryder.

"That she is. Got some rot, needs a lot of parts and loving care, but I think still worth the time for someone with energy and a desire to see it made whole again."

"Couldn't agree more," Colfax said. "That's real history sitting there. Right now, down in Boise at the Historical Institute, I have five interns who are graduate students in western history working to put together a Concord Coach we found buried in the hills."

Ryder nodded. "The old coach that vanished while on the Payette run back at the turn of the last century? You found it, huh?"

Anna looked at him. "Yeah, that's the one. How did you know about that?"

"One of the local mysteries," Ryder said. "My grandfather had harvest money on that coach when it vanished. When I heard about this coach down on the other side of town, I thought it might be the one that vanished. What got me excited about this beauty in the first place."

Colfax glanced at Anna. Now she had no idea what to think. Without that first coach vanishing in that robbery, Ryder would have never been interested in the coach in the first place.

Sometimes she felt that history was just making fun of her, and this was one of those times.

EIGHTEEN

September 18th, 2017
Boise, Idaho

COLFAX KNEW THAT they needed more information, if they could get it, from Ryder. So before talking about what Ryder wanted to do with the coach, he decided to try to work his way toward more information.

"I can understand why this Concord got you interested. You ought to see the grad students working on the one in Boise. They are so excited, the energy gets infectious. Did you ever go to college?"

"Oh, sure," Ryder said. "Dad said I was going to need all the education I

could get to run this place and he was right. He made me stop playing football and study. Can't say I liked him for that, but it turned out to be a damn right move."

Colfax laughed, but he had no idea what to say next. His mind was reeling. Somehow they had gotten a lot of information about Ryder very, very wrong.

He glanced at Anna. Her face had gone pale and it looked like she might be sick at any moment.

Luckily, Ryder kept talking, not noticing. "Met my wife in college, actually. Luckily, she loved this place and we moved back here to help out and then take over when Dad got sick. My mother helped us raise our kids, actually, until she passed a few years back."

Colfax just sort of stared at Ryder.

This was nothing at all to do with the information they had researched on this man.

History, Ryder's history, had changed.

Anna had her head down, staring at the dirt floor. She was breathing slowly.

How in the world could the information, their research, be so wrong? How could the history be so off?

"So you interested in the coach?" Ryder asked. "I know she's rough and all."

"Absolutely," Colfax said, yanking his attention back on the task at hand. "It will depend on price, of course."

Ryder waved his hand. "I don't need nothing for it. I'm going to be glad it gets to a good home is all."

"It will be combined with the one at the Historical Society to make a beautiful, like-new Concord Coach with all original parts. It will be on display for decades for people to see and appreciate. Can we at least give you credit for rescuing it?"

Ryder laughed. "That would be great, but give my entire family credit, not just me. My dad had to haul the thing here and put up with me trying to work on it. My kids loved it and used to play around it and in it. So make it from the entire Marks family of New Meadows and you got yourself a coach."

Colfax smiled and shook Ryder's strong, rough hand.

"Deal. I'll have the young kids with a large truck up here tomorrow afternoon to pick it up," Colfax said.

"Could we get a few more pieces of information from you?" Anna asked. "For the history of the coach. What were your father and mother's full names, your wife's name, and your children's names. We would like to have that for the story."

"And do you remember who exactly your dad bought it from?" Colfax asked. "And any history about how it got here? We really like all that sort of thing."

Ryder was more than happy to help them. More than happy, and they talked for the next forty minutes as Anna took notes.

Turned out the coach had been used for mail runs and transportation up into the small mining towns above McCall in the 1890s to early 1900s. It went to Warren, Edwardsburg, and Yellow Pine for almost twenty years before being retired from that route when all those towns fell into ghost town status.

After that the coach had been used up and down the valley between McCall and Cascade in parades and then for a time at a yearly fair for rides for kids. It made the kids too sick, so a rancher by the name of Caldwell bought it and stored it in his barn. When Ryder's dad saw it, he thought it would be a fun project for his son.

Colfax always found it sad how once proud parts of history faded. This Concord had been made with pride and served a function for almost a hundred years before being retired.

As the director of the Idaho Historical Institute, it was going to be great to have the Concord on display. Right there with all of its history.

But Anna didn't look so happy when Ryder gave her his wife's name and three children's names.

From what Colfax remembered, they were the names of the family that

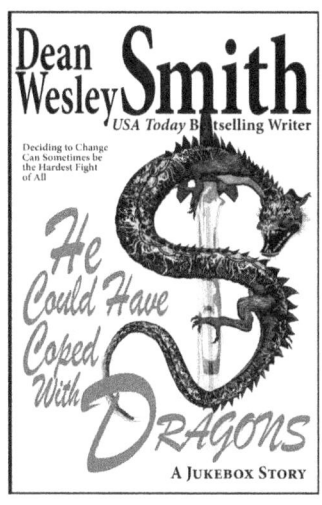

meant in the future anti-gravity would be invented.

After they thanked Ryder and were headed back out the long driveway, he turned to her. "Not the names you were expecting?"

"The exact names I was expecting," she said. "And that's the problem. Something else caused the split in timelines."

"So why did we think he married his childhood sweetheart and not go to college?" he asked. "How did we get that so wrong?"

"I honestly don't know," she said. "And that is bothering me more than anything else. I'm not even sure if he ever made that other decision."

NINETEEN

September 18th, 2017
Boise, Idaho

COLFAX CALLED THE interns and got them planning for the trip the next day, then he and Anna stopped at a nice restaurant in McCall for lunch.

The place looked out over the lake, had wooden tables and chairs, and a menu of sandwiches and soups like he had never seen before.

They both ordered turkey clubs and iced tea and then just sat looking out over the lake, thinking.

Outside the day was a perfect fall day and the colors of the leaves around the lake were starting to turn. It couldn't get any more beautiful than this, yet they sat there, not enjoying a bit of it.

Finally, he needed to ask some questions. The idea that history was not what they had researched bothered him as well. He depended on that research to be accurate. His entire job and life was based on history being accurate once researched carefully enough.

In this case, it hadn't been.

"So, a couple questions," he said. "Do you think we might have changed something in our time in 1902 to cause this kind of change in the timeline now?"

"I can't imagine what it would be," she said, shaking her head slowly. "But with history, as we are discovering in this case, the slightest detail different can sprout an infinite number of timelines. So maybe we did."

Colfax nodded. He had come to think over the years that this timeline was his "main" timeline, even though he knew that wasn't true. His base line was two hundred years in the future as well.

Duster had taken him forward to set his base there when he was first invited into the cavern and timeline jumping for research. Now, if something happened here in 2017, like a car wreck, he would just wake up in 2117 after only two minutes and fifteen seconds, and could come back.

Basically, for all intents and purposes, he and Anna were immortal. But since he had been originally born in this time, he thought of this timeline as his main one, even though it was nothing more than a crystal in a cave in 2117.

Colfax knew enough math about alternate timelines to know there was no main timeline.

Every timeline was a main timeline to those living in it.

"So right now, in this timeline," Colfax said, "we know Ryder went to college, got married, and his descendants invent antigravity for the world. Right?"

"I don't know that for sure," she said. "All my research seems to be shifting under us as we move along. Maybe our visit to his ranch to get the coach causes enough of a change down through time that things change in two hundred years. That is extreme math, with an infinite number of possibilities and timelines."

Colfax nodded. "So what exactly are we looking for at this point?"

"Nothing," she said. "That's the problem. I have to figure out a way to go back to square one on this project, anchor a point in time and in a timeline somewhere, and work the math from there back to different points in time in different timelines."

"Oh," he said.

He didn't much understand what she had said, but he didn't much like the sound of that. Not in the slightest.

That meant she was going to go timeline jumping. She had to and he would be useless to tag along.

"I'm going to need Bonnie and Duster's help on this," Anna said, staring out over the lake, "as well as Brice and Dixie. And the super computers in 2117."

He nodded.

"And the worst of this is that my entire project might not be possible. Simply by studying a fixed point in a timeline, I might be causing infinite alternate timelines to branch off."

Again, he nodded, being the best listener that he could, since timeline theory was her world, not his.

Brice and Dixie were two mathematicians that Bonnie and Duster had hired to be assistants. Colfax had heard Bonnie say once they were smarter than she and Duster.

So if Anna was going to need all four of their help on the math on this, it was

way, way, way beyond him, of that there was no doubt.

They ate pretty much in silence because he couldn't think of a damned thing to say to help her.

They then talked about what she needed to do when she got back to Boise to set up the meeting with the math core of the Institute.

About halfway back he said, "To make sure Ryder doesn't change his mind on the coach, I think I'll lead the crew back up here tomorrow."

She thought that was a good idea.

That night she fell asleep in his arms and the next morning, when his alarm went off, she was gone.

PART FOUR
No Time

TWENTY

September 20th, 2017
Boise, Idaho

ANNA KNEW THAT if she waited for Colfax to wake up, she might change her mind on what she had to do. Or worse yet, invite him along, something that would make him uncomfortable to say the least. This was her world, her specialty, not his.

Even though they didn't talk about it, they both knew she needed to go to 2117, get to work with Bonnie and Duster and Brice and Dixie and figure all this out.

She also knew that she could return in one afternoon as far as Colfax was concerned. To him, she would only be gone for a half-day or so. For her, she had no idea how long it was going to take.

And she hated that idea.

Completely hated it.

After she set the meeting up in 2117 with the others, she went to her own condo in 2117 to get changed. On one hand, it felt great to be home again, among her own things, in her own time.

On the other hand, it felt empty.

Very, very empty.

She had gotten so used to sharing things with Colfax.

Damn it all to hell, why did she have to fall in love?

Why did she miss him so damn much and she had only been gone a few hours.

Twice on the way to the meeting she almost cancelled to jump back and talk with Colfax.

Twice she kept going.

By the time she reached the meeting in a massive computer room in a cavern under the Institute, Bonnie took one look at her and asked, "Where's Colfax?"

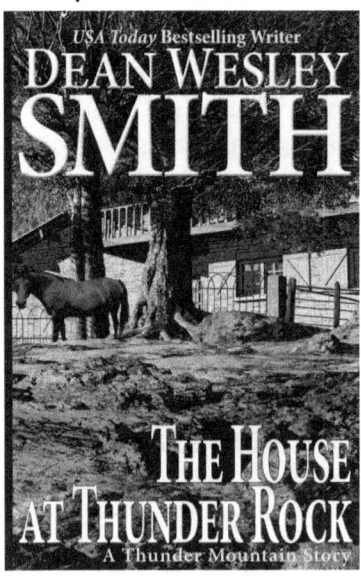

And to her horror, Anna broke into tears.

After Bonnie got her out to the kitchen area and calmed down a little, Anna told her that she had left Colfax this morning without saying goodbye because she didn't know what else to do. She knew this was going to take hundreds of years to solve. And she needed to have her focus and she knew this wasn't Colfax's world.

Bonnie just sat listening and when Anna was all done, she said simply, "Commute."

Anna had no idea what Bonnie was talking about.

Not a clue.

Bonnie actually laughed when she saw Anna's puzzled expression.

"For one of the smartest math minds I have had the pleasure to meet," Bonnie said, "sometimes you just miss the possibilities of what we are doing here. Just commute every day."

"Back to 2017?" Anna asked. That was something she had never once considered.

"Why not?" Bonnie asked. "That way Colfax can continue his research as well and commute back from the past when he is close enough to the Institute to do so."

Anna thought for a moment, the idea finally taking shape in her fuzzy mind.

"That would work, wouldn't it?"

Bonnie smiled. "Can't see why not. We don't have any other couples doing it. Director Parks and Kelli live all over the timelines. So who knows, you might start a trend."

With that Anna hugged Bonnie and went into the restroom to splash some cold water on her face, then joined the four others to try to start to figure out why history was changing as they observed it, spinning off new timelines, if that was what it was actually doing.

Now, thanks to Bonnie, Anna felt like this was going to be a fun project.

Six hours later, Anna went back to her apartment, got a bunch of clothing and supplies and things to work on for the evening, then headed back to the Institute.

She jumped to ten minutes after she had left. Then headed to Colfax's condo. By her time, she had only slipped out of bed just over forty minutes ago.

If she was lucky, she could make the man she loved some breakfast.

TWENTY-ONE

September 20th, 2017
Boise, Idaho

COLFAX ROLLED OVER and stared at the empty place in the bed. Anna belonged there. He knew why she had to leave.

He didn't like it at all, but he knew.

She knew she had to leave.

She really had no choice.

But now the question was could their love, the interest in each other survive the decades if not hundreds of years it was going to take her to work on that project and find the answers.

He had no idea.

He stood in the shower for the longest time, trying to get past the deep, deep feeling of loss.

That might never be possible.

Then, as he got out of the shower, the wonderful smell of cooking bacon hit him.

She couldn't be back, could she?

Of course she could.

What an idiot he was. For her, hundreds of years might have passed since she crawled out of bed this morning.

He got dressed, trying to not make anything up about what kind of person Anna would be when he went down there. Had all the years changed her so that she didn't love him anymore?

For someone as smart as he was, he could sure be stupid about being in love.

Finally, he got up enough courage to go down the stairs.

She was standing with her back to him in the modern condo kitchen. Her bright red hair was up on her head as normal. She had on jeans and a light-blue silk blouse that complemented her hair and skin.

She looked wonderful. So good he could hardly breathe.

She turned from the stove, saw him coming down the stairs, and beamed. "Thought I was going to have to either eat all this myself or wake you up with breakfast in bed."

"Damn," he said, smiling at her as he hit the bottom of the stairs and pretended to start back up. "Got up too soon."

She laughed and then came out of the kitchen and into his arms and kissed him.

She felt like the same woman completely. But he had to know.

"How long?"

"Longest damn eight hours of my life," she said, finishing putting the eggs on the plates and then some bacon.

He almost choked.

"Eight hours?"

"Had a meeting in 2117 with the math folks," she said.

She pointed to a chair for him to sit at the dining room table that looked out through a patio door over the grass lawn and the Boise River beyond. Then she put a glass of orange juice in front of him along with a plate covered with bacon, eggs, and toast. What a wonderful breakfast.

It smelled heavenly. And he was hungry, but instead he just kept staring at her.

"It was sort of embarrassing to start," she said. "We both know that this project I have to tackle is going to take a lot of years. Maybe decades or more."

He nodded.

She smiled and shook her head. "So when Bonnie asked me where you were, I broke down into tears."

He stood up and moved around the table and just hugged her.

After a moment, she kissed him long and hard, then pointed to his plate. "Eat before it gets cold."

He moved back over and sat down.

"It seems," she said, "that in these short months, I have fallen completely and totally and madly in love with you."

He wanted to stand up and hug and kiss her again, but instead said, "I have done the same with you."

"Well," she said, "we are a pair. Our work takes us hundreds of years apart in opposite directions in time."

He nodded. "That's our problem."

Her mood seemed so light, it was clear she had a solution. He just couldn't imagine what it might be.

"So when I told Bonnie I didn't want to be away from you for all that time, she managed to not laugh, called me the dumbest smart person she had ever met, and just said we should commute."

"Commute?" Colfax asked.

He had no clue at all what she meant.

"It's a well-duh for me," Anna said, "since I understand all this timeline stuff. But I never needed to think about this kind of thing before I fell in love with you."

His mind was reeling. "Going to have to explain commute to a guy used to the Old West and riding very slow horses."

"Every night I simply come back to this time," she said, smiling at him. "We maybe stay here or get a house together."

He just looked at her, stunned.

She laughed. "I'm going to be in the Institute anyway. So like today, I had a long meeting and then got back here in time to cook you breakfast."

"Will that work?" he asked, still struggling to understand it.

"Completely," she said. "The problem is when you are back in the past, you will be away from the Institute. But you can still be here for dinner every evening as well, even if you are away for months at a time back there. We can have a regular life here. The future and the past are just our offices, in a manner of speaking. Places we commute to."

Finally it all clicked into place.

That would work.

He wasn't going to lose Anna.

In fact, he might be able to help her.

And every night in this timeline, they could be together, talking, making love, sharing their work.

He got up again from his chair, moved over and kissed her one more time, long and hard.

Then when the kiss broke, he said simply, "Thank you. You saved me from hundreds of years roaming the Old West as a tragic, lonely figure, slouching on my horse, drifting from town to town."

She laughed. "Had it all planned out, huh?"

"Too vivid an imagination," he said.

She laughed and pushed him back to his breakfast. "Eat up, we got some planning to do and I got to get some sleep, since I have already been going for most of a day. We'll need to get our days worked out as well."

Damn he liked the sound of the idea they were planning to do.

He liked the word "they" in that sentence more than anything else.

TWENTY-TWO

September 20th, 2017
Boise, Idaho

ANNA WAS SOUND asleep in Colfax's bed when he gently nudged her.

Could she have already slept eight hours? She still felt tired.

At breakfast they had decided that he would go ahead and go with his interns back to the Marks ranch to get the coach, just to make sure things stayed smooth with Ryder Marks.

He figured he would be gone a total of six-seven hours, more than enough time for her to get some real sleep.

"Sorry to wake you early," Colfax said, his voice gentle.

She opened one eye. "How long?"

"You've been asleep for just over an hour," he said.

She nodded, realizing that if he was waking her, they had a problem.

She said, "Give me a minute."

She climbed out of bed, went to the bathroom, splashed cold water on her face, put on a bathrobe, and came back out.

"So what happened?" she asked.

"No coach," he said simply.

She shook her head, not understanding at all what he had just said.

"Better repeat that."

"No coaches, actually," Colfax said, sitting on the edge of the bed, looking at her with the most worried look she had

ever seen. "I got to the Historical Society and they weren't working on any coach and thought I was nuts to ask. So I called Ryder Marks and he didn't know me either and doesn't have a coach in his barn. Although he was pretty sure that old man Campbell on the other side of New Meadows had one."

Now she was awake.

Completely and totally awake.

"Make us each a cup of coffee to go," she said, "while I get dressed. We got to find Bonnie and Duster."

He nodded and headed down the stairs.

What he had told her wasn't possible.

It flat wasn't possible.

Yet it had happened, which meant they were now in another timeline. Her coming back here or something they did yesterday had shifted timelines under them. She knew that was possible, that it had happened before. But she had no idea why now, with these stupid stagecoaches.

She took a deep breath. Given time, this could all be explained with math. She knew that.

But Colfax had looked shaken.

She got dressed and was down the stairs before Colfax had the coffee ready. She had him repeat exactly what he had told her, just to make sure.

"What could cause this?" he asked.

"We have slipped to a timeline, or our old timeline merged with a timeline, where the coaches never existed in the way we knew of them," she said. "How or why, I have no idea."

That idea bothered her. Something must have happened far larger than she had thought possible. But, of course, with history, often the largest things were very small in detail.

They walked quickly along the Boise River Parkway the half-mile to the Institute. They found Director Parks in his office and had him put in an emergency call to Bonnie and Duster.

Thirty minutes later the four of them were in the large cavern. Bonnie and Duster were sitting at the kitchen counter, Anna and Colfax stood behind the counter, leaning up against the stove and fridge.

Then, Colfax told Bonnie and Duster what had happened.

Both of them looked stunned.

Anna felt stunned hearing it again.

"Call the Historical Society again," Duster said. "Make sure one of your interns isn't doing some sort of sick joke on you."

"I went there," Colfax said. "They are not. It wouldn't even be possible considering where they were working on that coach and what is there now. And I checked all incoming records and no record at all of the coach coming in and the Historical Society working on the dig."

"That coach has yet to be found on that hill in this timeline," Anna said, "if it actually ever ended up on that hill."

"We've slipped timelines," Bonnie said softly. "Actually, the timeline changed under us."

"I didn't feel the normal shimmering," Duster said.

"Shimmering?" Colfax asked a half second before Anna could.

"We discovered that by making certain changes to decisions, often major changes," Bonnie said, "but in minor ways, it cancels out timelines, makes them blend into others."

"Can you explain why that would even happen?" Colfax asked.

Duster nodded. "An infinite number of timelines split off and are formed from

every happening, every decision that has more than one possible outcome."

Colfax knew that much.

"If a timeline doesn't become a certain distinct level of difference from the one it split from, the rules of conservation of time, energy, and mass take over and the new timelines merge back with the original one. The new ones cease to exist."

Colfax nodded.

"So," Bonnie said, "if that happens to cause timelines to no longer need to exist after a long period of time, they blur back into each other and there is a shimmering sensation like a wave of heat passing over."

"We're still working on the math of it all," Duster said. "Looks like that math just hit the priority spot."

Anna only nodded.

"So why do we still remember the coaches and such, the way it was before the merge?" Colfax asked.

Anna thought that a very good question, actually, one she did not know the answer to.

"We are not from this timeline," Duster said. "All four of us are technically travelers here from the future. Even though three of us were born in this time. Just not this timeline. So we are outside the change and would remember it."

Anna nodded. That made complete sense.

"So what kind of major thing could cause this?" Colfax asked.

"Timelines that had existed for awhile and instead of growing apart were coming back together," Bonnie said. "Think of a river going around a very large rock. At one point there are two flows moving away from each other, then they come back together."

"It was slipping before this morning," Anna said, suddenly realizing what they were saying. "Merging if you will. Our research data was wrong about Ryder Marks, even though we had both checked it and I had checked it from the future."

Bonnie nodded. "Time was adjusting the unimportant details."

"Before that," Colfax said. "When we thought the coach that ended up on the hill was the same one in New Meadows. Turned out it wasn't."

Duster looked at the two of them and nodded. "That water around a rock analogy really works. Those were signs the timelines were as far apart as they were going to get and were coming back together."

Anna agreed completely. Now so much of this made sense.

"We are the only common element, aren't we?" Anna asked. "Colfax and I meeting is when this all started to merge."

Both Bonnie and Duster shrugged.

"It might be the focus on one detail in time," Bonnie said, "that cleaned up a bunch of small things that kept the timelines apart."

"But I doubt two travelers, not changing much of anything, could cause this," Duster said. "It was natural and we have theories it happens all the time. We just have never had anyone observing it before."

Anna nodded. That made more sense then them changing entire timelines.

That would take more years of math to figure out for sure.

Then Bonnie and Duster stood.

"You two stay right here, in this cavern. Bonnie and I will be back in ten minutes. We're going to run forward, see what we can see."

Anna nodded.

She looked at Colfax, the man she loved more than anything.

He looked worried.

Very worried.

And so was she.

And she had a hunch they were both worried about the same thing. Were the changes done, or were the changes going to make it so that they never met?

Anna hoped they could get an answer to that one very quickly.

TWENTY-THREE

September 20th, 2017
Boise, Idaho

COLFAX AND ANNA sat at the bar for the fifteen minutes it took Bonnie and Duster to run forward in time and check out a number of alternate timelines. They held hands while finishing their coffees.

In all his life he had never been so shocked when his interns didn't know about the coach. His stomach had been twisting and he wanted to kick something when he got to the Historical Society and the coach wasn't there.

He flat didn't understand timelines enough to even begin to understand what was happening, even though Bonnie and Duster had done a pretty good job of describing it.

But he did know that his entire life suddenly felt very shallow.

He had been given this incredible chance to go back into history and research, get details right in his books, learn the real facts.

But now history was just shifting and with it his entire belief system.

Bonnie and Duster came back into the large cavern and stopped near the door.

Duster waved them over. "Show us the crystals you two have been using."

Colfax and Anna got off the bar stools and followed Bonnie and Duster back into the stairwell.

"Everything all right in the future?" Colfax asked.

"Far as we could tell," Bonnie said. "No one felt a shimmering or noticed any differences, including other historians. So it seems to be focused around the timelines that affect those two stagecoaches for some reason."

They went through the supply room and down a long hallway with maybe a hundred doors along the right side. Behind each door was a long narrow cave cut out of the rock. On each side were hundreds of crystals. Each crystal was a timeline.

Colfax knew that right now Bonnie and Duster and he and Anna were in different timelines, actually. Bonnie and Duster had come back from 2117 through one or two crystals, Anna had just come back to this timeline through another, and Colfax through another.

At the start, he and Anna had gone into the past through different timelines, then matched up here and gone back through the same crystal for the stage ride.

But in theory, the thousands and thousands of crystals in these caves should be from timelines so close as to be impossible to tell them apart. They had been taken from the nexus in a very small area and if any changes anyone in the Institute made in a past to cause a new infinite number of timelines to form, those new crystals for the new timelines formed in the nexus.

That was just about as much as Colfax knew as a historian.

"Show us the crystal you both went back through to ride the coach," Bonnie said.

They went four doors down the hallway and opened up the large door there, then went in.

The hundreds and hundreds of crystals lit up the long, narrow room with pink light. The tables and wooden boxes were fine down the middle, and the wire fences looked fine.

Colfax went down the long room to about a three-quarters place and pointed to what was now an empty spot in the wall.

There had been a crystal there.

An entire timeline.

"What happened?" he asked, glancing at Anna, then at Bonnie and Duster.

Anna touched his arm in a reassuring way and said, "It blended with another timeline because it no longer had any differences from a parent timeline. Therefore it had no reason to exist and vanished."

Duster pointed to a bunch of empty holes in the rocks toward the back of the room. "Looks like we need to have another visit to the nexus, get more timelines."

"Is this the first time this has ever happened?" Anna asked.

"No," Bonnie said. "But we were traveling out of the nexus at that point and couldn't tell how much the crystals were disturbed."

"I'll get Parks down here and we'll do an inventory of how many we are going to need, both in this area and in the other areas. And see if this affected any crystals in the future Institute rooms. Then we'll make some plans on how to harvest more. We haven't taken a crystal from the nexus since 1885."

"Seems logical that this would happen at some point," Bonnie said.

Colfax nodded. He honestly had no idea what was happening, but the three mathematicians were treating him like he did, so better to not remind them he was a historian, not a math geek.

"We caused the last one on purpose," Bonnie said. "It's going to take some time and study to figure out what caused this one. I hope you kept good notes about what was in that timeline and what will have changed in others, besides the coaches."

Colfax nodded. "They are good. Very good."

"And we're going to need to get other historians with you matching notes," Duster said. "The detail that caused this merging back of timelines will be small, but it will be important for us to understand."

"Anna," Bonnie said, turning back for the door. "You will take point on the math side of this. Colfax, you get point on the historical side."

Colfax looked at Anna and smiled.

Now he felt better. The mathematicians who knew what had happened were treating this as another study project. From the historical side, he could as well.

He would just have to keep reminding himself that history is never solid. He knew that in school, forgot it when he started traveling in time. When you can touch history, it often felt solid.

Anna smiled back, and then hand in hand they followed Bonnie and Duster out of the cavern.

PART FIVE
Repeating History

TWENTY-FOUR

October 19th, 2017
Boise, Idaho

ANNA WAS SURPRISED to learn after one month of work and inventory that over six hundred crystals had vanished from the caverns. Six hundred timelines had merged back into parent timelines.

Anna's project no longer was to study points in time, but how timelines merged. And figure out, as much as possible, why the last timeline merge happened.

Her math, in one month, along with the help of the Institute's four other major mathematicians, showed that this merging was a far more common occurrence than they had thought.

The only reason no one had noticed it before in the Institute was the fact that there were hundreds of thousands of crystals in the Institute over four hundred years. But those crystals were such a tiny, tiny insignificant part of the infinite number of crystals in the nexus. So if a merge happened once in four hundred years in this small a sampling, it meant a merge happened all the time through the mass of the nexus.

Timelines were being formed and flowing back together continuously.

And she was very glad to see on one trip forward, that the merge had made the invention of anti-gravity an almost certainty, at least in the timelines she could jump to.

That cleared that out of her mind.

And now her focus was on the math, and spending the evenings with Colfax. Both of them, at first, had worried that the merge would take them apart. But Bonnie had finally assured her with math that the chance of that happening was so minute as to not be calculated.

Relief didn't begin to describe that.

Also, over the last month, she and the other four mathematicians had determined with math that the Concord Coach had something to do with the turning point in those timelines.

But that was as close as the numbers could get them.

It was Duster who finally said, "Looks like we are in the field on this one."

He meant that until they found the detail in history that caused the difference and the merge back, they would get no closer to answers.

So it was time again for Anna to get into the past with Colfax. Part of that flat scared her, part of that she was excited about.

So on a chilly morning in late October, she and Colfax left their apartment and walked along the river in the cool breeze

to the Institute. Then they headed down to the crystals and jumped back to October 22nd, 1902.

And once again got ready to head out in two days to see if the brothers robbed the stage again.

This time, she brought an extra pair of complete thermal underwear and an extra sweater, all modern designed but made to look like it belonged in 1902, just in case.

And for two days, they enjoyed the big feather bed and she cooked peanut butter cookies in the cavern while they worked, often in silence, around the large fireplace.

TWENTY-FIVE

October 24th, 1902
Boise, Idaho

COLFAX SET UP HIS camera and binoculars across from the corner on the old Kelton Road, in the exact same place he and Anna had set up before.

She was beside him and this time both of them had dressed warmer for the bone-chilling cold of the morning along the Boise River.

"I'm set," she said.

"So am I," he said.

He loved that the two of them were back here again. Over the last month he had spent a lot of time checking on different aspects of his notes, sometimes traveling for a month before returning for dinner. They had dinner together every night in 2017, no matter how long she was in the future or he was in the past.

And that was working out wonderfully so far. He felt closer to her than he'd thought possible and they shared everything.

So far, all the details from his historical research had been accurate. The timeline merges hadn't affected anything, which made him feel much better about his chosen profession. It seems that only the stagecoaches were the turning points, as far as he and other historians in the Institute could see from checking notes.

And the math side had come to the same conclusion. Events around the two stagecoaches were where these timelines had broken apart and then merged back together.

After the merge of timelines, they were not sure if the coach robbery would take place or not. They were now in the field, as Duster called it, gathering information.

"Not sure I want to watch this for a third time," Anna said.

Colfax nodded to that. After dying in the robbery once, he didn't really want to watch it either. But they needed to watch and record it in order to see if something was slightly different.

"Here come the brothers," Anna said.

He turned to see that the two brothers were riding up the trail in the opposite direction the stage would be coming. Just as they had done the first time they watched.

When the brothers got to where the trail crossed over Dry Creek, they tied up their horses and kept going on foot.

"Stage," Anna whispered a moment later.

Colfax's stomach twisted as he turned to his camera.

He could see the Thorpe brothers' faces clearly and both of them had their hands on their guns sticking out of their belts.

The stage came into sight and the brothers took out their guns.

So far, everything was the same. Exactly.

Adams slowed the stage and stopped as he had done when they were inside. Then he got down on the side of the road, toward the brothers.

What seemed like an eternity later, Adams was behind the large coach when suddenly a shot echoed over the valley.

A moment later Danny Thorpe dragged Adams' body around the back of the coach and off the edge of the road, rolling it down toward the outcropping of rocks below.

Danny followed the rolling body until it stopped, then took it around the rocks and stuffed it into the crevice.

Something didn't seem right to Colfax.

Something felt different.

He watched as Billy Thorpe took the stage up to the top of the hill, undid the horses, and when the second brother got there, they pushed the coach down into the ravine and went to cover it up.

Then, just as before, the two brothers rode away from the site with the horses.

"Shit," Anna said. "I really didn't want to see that again."

He glanced at her. She was clearly shaken, her face pale under the hat she had pulled down over her head and ears.

"I didn't either," Colfax said. "But something felt different about this time."

Anna nodded. "I noticed that as well, but not sure if it's because that's the third time I've seen it from one angle or another or not. I'm still not past getting killed up on that road."

"In a timeline that no longer exists," Colfax said.

"What I remember most," Anna said as she worked to take her camera and tripod apart, "was how loud those shots were."

Colfax instantly knew what was different.

"Adams was only shot once this time," he said.

Anna's bright green eyes were round as she looked at Colfax, then back at the rock crevice where they had stuffed Adam's body.

"Could he still be alive?" she asked, clearly to herself.

Colfax quickly put his camera and tripod back together and got it focused on the crevice and the road above.

Anna did the same thing.

And ten long and painful minutes later, Adams crawled out of the crevice and braced himself on a rock, holding his stomach. Blood was black on his shirt and coat, but he seemed to be breathing solidly. There was no doubt he was in a lot of pain, though.

Then as they watched, wanting to help, but not daring to move a muscle, he crawled back up the steep hillside to the old road.

Crawled, not walked.

Crawled.

TWENTY-SIX

October 24th, 1902
Boise, Idaho

ANNA COULDN'T BELIEVE that they might have found the difference in all the timelines.

A single shot.

One way a man dies, the other he lives.

She so wanted to go to help him, but she knew they didn't belong here. And if they were going to get real answers to the mystery of the timelines, they needed to stay out of the timeline events completely.

In any other time or place, both she and Colfax would have rushed to Adams' aide. But now they couldn't.

And that felt horrible.

Almost as bad as getting shot up on that road had felt.

They stayed in place, recording, not even talking.

Anna was so in shock and her stomach was so twisted up, she could hardly feel the cold wind and light blowing snow.

Every five minutes, Adams would stand, walk about ten steps, turn around, walk back, and then drop to the road again.

"Why is he doing that?" Anna asked after the second time.

"Keeping from freezing to death," Colfax said. "You have to move, but he is clearly losing blood from the wound, so if someone doesn't find him pretty soon, he's doomed."

She didn't like the sound of that. The idea that they would just stand out here in the trees and watch a man die slowly was abhorrent to her. But she could see no choice at the moment.

Sometimes she hated being a time traveler. Just hated it and this was one of those times.

Finally, about thirty minutes after Adams had reached the road, a buggy pulled by one horse, driven by what looked to be a clergyman came along the road.

Adam sat up and then managed to stand.

The guy, shot through the stomach, was clearly as strong as anyone she had ever seen.

The buggy stopped and the man, clearly a priest or preacher of some sort, ran to Adams' aide.

"He's going to get medical help," Colfax said. "Preachers and nuns in this time and in the West were like field medics in a war. They did most of the doctoring."

Anna nodded. That was a fact she didn't know.

They watched without moving as the preacher got Adams to the back seat in the buggy, then checked his wound and had Adams press a cloth against the wound.

Both she and Colfax got lots of pictures of the preacher. Then, instead of going back toward Boise, the preacher went forward.

"Why are they going that way?" Anna asked.

"Closest small hospital from here in this time is between Nampa and Caldwell," Colfax said. "He's going to cross the river and go directly across the valley. About twice as close as going back to Boise would be."

Anna just nodded and hoped Adams could survive the rough ride.

When the buggy got out of sight, Colfax started to pack up his camera and tripod.

Anna just stood there, staring at the hillside. She was so numb, both from the cold and the events, she didn't know if she could move.

Colfax came over and put his arm around her, which felt wonderful. "Come on, math girl, we got a ton of research and calculations to do."

She nodded. "Just hard to fathom we saw two different timelines here with the same event."

"Three," Colfax said. "Our bodies were in that crevice in one, remember?"

She laughed. "Damn tough to forget."

With that she started packing up.

They stopped in the Idanha Hotel for a wonderful lunch of warm beef soup and melt-in-your-mouth bread that made her feel a ton better. Then they made it back to the Institute by three in the afternoon.

They took a hot shower together, then crawled up in the wonderful feather bed for a long nap.

When she awoke two hours later, Colfax was gone.

A note on the pillow said, "Downstairs eating your cookies."

She laughed and twenty minutes later joined him.

And from there, after making sure they had all their gear with them, they headed back to 2017 and the historical records of the hospitals of the time.

They had a lead.

Neither of them knew where it might go.

TWENTY-SEVEN

October 23rd, 2017
Boise, Idaho

COLFAX AND ANNA couldn't find any records at all from the Sisters of Mercy Hospital between Nampa and Caldwell, where the pastor would have taken Adams. The entire hospital didn't even have a real building until 1910 and it burnt down in 2005, losing most historical records in the process.

But they did find some court records of Canyon County where the two brothers were arrested, tried for robbery and murder, convicted, and hung.

Anna actually cheered when they found that detail. Said it made her feel better as a victim of those two cold-blooded killers.

But it also meant that Adams died after he identified them as his killers. And that made her sad.

Colfax just nodded when she said something. "A gut shot in the Old West was almost always fatal. Problem was it took a long time to die, usually from the infections."

She could understand that. Didn't like the idea, but understood it.

The two brothers never bought their ranch and the mailbags that Adams had been delivering reached their intended people about a month late.

The robbery was only a footnote in history as one of the last stagecoach robberies, because the last stagecoach robbery was in 1915, thirteen years later.

It seemed, from what Anna and Duster and Bonnie could work with the math, they had found their one detail.

Bonnie and Duster both agreed. That second gunshot had made all the difference and they would never know why the brother hadn't taken it.

And all the timelines where he did take that second shot had merged away into timelines where he didn't take it.

Anna had discovered that the actual merge point wasn't around the stagecoaches, but two hundred years later. Even with the ranch and the success of future generations, the Thorpe family ended up making no difference at all to history.

So the merge of timelines was around the year 2200, over three hundred years after not taking the second shot. And that was why no one really felt any sort of shimmering. The merge of timelines wasn't in any way important. Just normal timeline stuff.

Four days after being back in 2017, she and Colfax were sitting in the Brooks Garden Restaurant, in their favorite booth clear to the back amid all the plants. The wonderful smell of garlic bread sticks filled the air and they had already take care of a half a basket full of them.

Outside, the air felt like it was turning toward winter and the leaves on the trees were all turning spectacular colors of reds, oranges, and browns. Boise was a city of trees, with most streets under canopies of limbs, and when fall hit, there was no place more beautiful on the planet.

They had walked the mile from the Institute to the restaurant for lunch, just reveling in the wonderful day.

"I'm going to head back tomorrow morning to 1902," Colfax said. "I want to put a bow on all this by finding out exactly what happened with Adams."

She munched on a garlic stick, nodding. She thought that was a very good idea, actually.

"You want to come along?" he asked, smiling.

She looked at him. "I have seen images of hospital tents in the Civil War. Is this going to be better?"

He shook his head. "No, not much."

"Then," she said, smiling and taking another breadstick, "I think I'll just work on some calculations and keep the images of these wonderful trees and the taste of this wonderful breadstick in my memory instead."

He laughed. "I can't say that I blame you. But when I get back tomorrow morning, you want to go help me *discover* a stagecoach?"

"Snakes?" she asked, smiling at him.

"Too cold," he said, laughing.

"Then I would love to."

TWENTY-EIGHT

October 26th, 1902
Boise, Idaho

COLFAX WENT BACK to 1902 through the same crystal that he and Anna had witnessed Adams save himself, but arrived a full day after they had left.

They had left some peanut butter cookies on the table in the cavern near the kitchen and a few of them were still there, along with a note from another traveler saying, "Thanks. Make more."

Colfax chuckled at that. Then he got prepared for the ride to the Nampa Caldwell area. The threat of snow had lifted but it was still cold out, unseasonably cold.

He took his time on the ride, stopping in a hotel in Nampa for the night before going the last few miles to the hospital site. He kept the reservation on the room

because it actually had an indoor bath down the hallway upstairs and for an extra few bucks he could get hot water for the tub. He was going to need it, he had no doubt.

The hospital was in a farmhouse just down a narrow line of trees off the main road between Nampa and Caldwell.

A number of large, white, military-style tents littered the area to one side of the hospital along with three outhouses. Colfax knew from what little bit he could find about this hospital at this point in time that the nuns that ran the hospital lived in the tents year-round.

He opened the large front door to the building and was hit by a blast of too-warm air and the smell of flesh rotting, mixed with the thick smell of shit and pee.

He wanted to just turn around and go back out in to the fresh air, but he made himself stop and his stomach settle. He had brought an extra set of clothes and a different coat and boots because he knew

this smell was not something he would ever get out of anything. He had been in these places before in this time period.

It was because of places like this that entire generations believed that hospitals were places you went to die. There was absolute truth in that at this point in history. Very few patients came out of these places alive.

In the modern world, these would be more like hospices, to help ease the pain and suffering of those who were dying.

In front of him in the wide-open main floor of the house, he could see ten beds. More than likely there were more up the narrow staircase on the back wall.

Beside one bed, a man with a badge sat with a notebook, talking to the man in the bed.

Colfax saw that the man was Adams. His skin was pale and he looked tired, but he seemed to be talking normally.

One of the nuns sat on the other side of the bed from the sheriff, also taking notes.

The sheriff knew Adams wasn't going to make it, so he was taking his story down, with a nun doing the same thing. Having a nun testify in court as to what Adams said before he died would certainly help put the brothers into the gallows.

And clearly the sheriff's smart thinking had worked, since both brothers would be hung for Adam's murder in two years in the Idaho State Penitentiary out Warm Springs Avenue about a mile from the Institute.

Colfax stood and watched for a few minutes until another nun who seemed to be about sixty came up to ask him if there was someone he was looking for.

Colfax shook his head. "I just came to make a donation to his hospital, if I could."

She smiled a grandmother toothless smile and said, "That would be very kind. All help is welcome."

He had prepared for this and had five hundred dollars in his pocket in an envelope. More than a full year of income for this small facility.

He pulled it out and handed it to the nun. "Keep doing great work."

With one last look at Adams, he turned and headed for the door. He had seen all he needed to see.

Before the nun could open the envelope and make a big deal about the donation, he thanked her and went out the door into the cold, fresh fall afternoon.

He needed a bath desperately.

It was going to be a long, smelly ride back to his hotel in Nampa.

Very long.

TWENTY-NINE

October 24th, 2017
Boise, Idaho

ANNA STOOD BESIDE Colfax in almost the exact spot they had been shot in a timeline that now no longer existed.

The stress of being here still made her tense. She still had a vivid memory of that coach and those two men with guns and Colfax lying on the road bleeding.

That was an image she doubted would ever leave her mind, even if it actually never happened in any timeline. It happened to her and Colfax and that to her was all that mattered.

Up the gully above the old road, four interns from the Idaho State Historical

Society were digging into the hill where the Concord Coach should be.

The air was chilly, but not too cold and from the old road she could see out over the river and the Treasure Valley. Including down to the spot where twice they had stood in the trees and filmed this corner.

Everything was in fall colors and the sight was beautiful, so she focused on that instead of where they had stood.

She had watched earlier as Colfax presented his research to the five grad-student interns at the Historical Society about the old stage robbery, how the driver had died in the hospital, how the robbers had hung for murder.

And then he had asked them how many of them wanted to see if they could find the old stagecoach.

He pretended, when they got there, to go through the robbery from what he had dug up in the records from Adams' dying testimony, from the shooting of Adams and putting him down the hill, to him climbing back up and being rescued by a pastor.

"If you were the two killers," Colfax said, "what would you do with a stage from here if you didn't dare be seen with it?"

Anna was impressed that two of the interns figured out almost instantly where the stage would be.

They had been digging in the rocks and dirt up the narrow gulch now for thirty minutes and no luck so far. Colfax had smiled at her when she said it was taking some time.

"These students are trained to dig without hurting anything they might find," he said. "That takes longer."

And that to her made complete sense.

She had been so sheltered in her math world that she was always learning things in Colfax's world, and she liked that.

It was only five minutes later that one of the interns yelled that they had something.

Anna went with Colfax up the gully to where the interns had dug out one of the side-panels of the old Concord stage.

"Well," Colfax said. "Ain't she a beauty."

Anna had never seen five grad students so excited. And yet, at the same time, so careful.

Colfax supervised them for a short time, then told the grad student in charge where in the Historical Society to clear out for the coach. Then he turned to Anna and smiled. "I've got a lead on another one as well."

"For parts?" one of the grad students asked. "If you could get another one, we could make one original Concord Coach perfect, I'm sure."

Colfax laughed. "I'll see what I can do. Call me if you need anything."

With that, Anna followed him back down the gulch, picking their way over rocks to where they had parked the Institute's Cadillac.

"You up for a wonderful day off, driving north to see about the other stage? This time of the year it is stunning up there."

She looked at him and smiled. "Shore Lodge Resort, dinner, soaking in one of those fantastic pools?"

"Don't forget the soft bed overlooking the lake," he said, smiling.

"Get a reservation," she said.

"Already got it," he said smiling back at her. "And Campbell, who owns the old Concord, is very happy to talk with us in the morning."

"Pretty sure of yourself, aren't you?" she asked, looking up into those handsome brown eyes and smiling face.

"Just starting to know the woman I love," he said. "She likes roughing it, but no lower than a four-star hotel."

She laughed and reached up and kissed him, pulling his head down to her level.

Then when she let him go, she said, "I was so hoping you would figure that out."

"So," he asked, "can a historian who loves 1902 make it with a mathematician who loves big computing power from 2117?"

She laughed. "I'll show you the answer to that up close and personal in that big bed in Shore Lodge."

"Damn," he said, pretending to fan himself. "How's a guy supposed to drive the speed limit now?"

She laughed, gave him a long hug and kiss.

Then they turned away from where they had been killed on that old road toward a wonderful future together in a bunch of different timelines.

Timelines they both hoped would stick around a very long time.

Coming Next Issue in *Smith's Monthly*

#1...October 2013

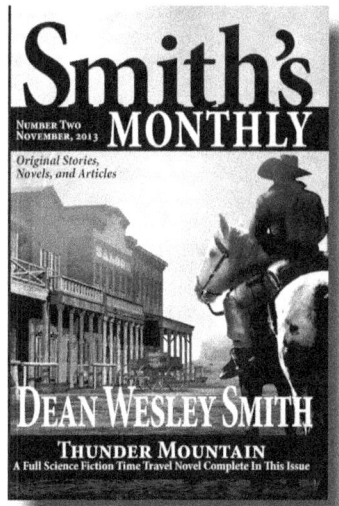

#2...November 2013

#3...December 2013

#4...January 2014

#5...February 2014

#6...March 2014

#7...April 2014

#8...May 2014

#9...June 2014

#10...July 2014

#11...August 2014

#12...September 2014

#13...October 2014

#14...November 2014

#15...December 2014

#16...January 2015

#17...February 2015

#18...March 2015

#19...April 2015

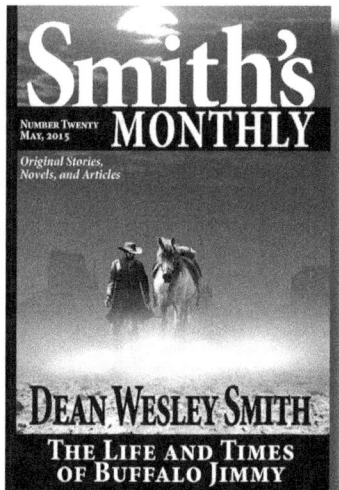

#20...May 2015

#21...June 2015

#22...July 2015

#23...August 2015

#24...September 2015

#25...October 2015

#26...November 2015

#27...December 2015

#28...January 2016

#29...February 2016

#30...March 2016

#31...April 2016

#32...May 2016

#33...June 2016

#34...July 2016

#35...August 2016

#36...September 2016

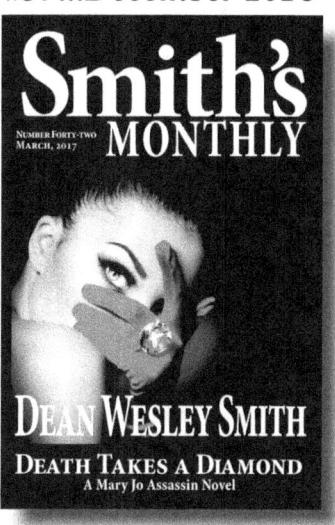

Thank You!!

I would like to thank the following wonderful people who support my blog and my work through Patreon. Your support is very important to me. Thanks!

Irette Y Patterson
Kathryn Rooney
Erick Lindman
Christopher Ridge
Raphael Husbands
James Gotaas
milady133
Danica Oakley
Kenny Norris
Kate MacLeod
Leah Cutter
Leigh Anderson
Robert J. McCarter
Jennette Heikes
Jamie Curierre
Albert Lemke
Marsha Kessler
Diane Darcy
Robin Brande
James Husum
Terry Mixon
Shantnu Tiwari
Chong Go
Maria Grace
Gnondpom
David Hendrickson
Fen

Sherman Cox
Miguel Angel Alonso Pulido
Marian Goldeen
Michelle Tatam
J.R. Murdock
Gunnar Gunderson
Jesse P Thurston
coraa
Martin Barkawitz
David Beers
Leslie Claire Walker
Nancy Hendrickson
F.I. Goldhaber
Michael J Lawrence
Barbara G. Tarn
Anthony St. Clair
Ann Tucker
Karl Gallagher
T. Thorn Coyle
Cristof Jones Harrison
Tasha Turner Lennhoff
Brenda Smith
Kari Wolfe
Mary Jo Rabe

And a very special thank you to Betsey Wilcox.

www.ingramcontent.com/pod-product-compliance
Lightning Source LLC
Chambersburg PA
CBHW081155170626
46813CB00009B/3199